WARDEN

THE VIGILANTE CHRONICLES™ BOOK THREE

NATALIE GREY
MICHAEL ANDERLE

DISRUPTIVE IMAGINATION®

LMBPN Publishing
PMB 196, 2540 South Maryland Pkwy
Las Vegas, NV 89109

First US edition, July 2018
Version 1.03, August 2018

WARDEN TEAM

Thanks to the JIT Readers

Daniel Weigert
Mary Morris
James Caplan
John Ashmore
Peter Manis
Micky Cocker

If We've missed anyone, please let us know!

Editor
Lynne Stiegler

From Natalie

For M and T

From Michael

To Family, Friends and
Those Who Love
To Read.
May We All Enjoy Grace
To Live The Life We Are
Called.

Yofu image by Eric Quigley

S weat dripped into Gar's eyes, and he winced in pain. His whole body ached. Things he hadn't known existed ached. Could internal organs ache? His did.

He had to focus on the *real* threat, however.

"I told you two I was uncomfortable with this." He looked at Barnabas and Shinigami, who were playing chess in the corner. Both Barnabas and Shinigami's avatar sat cross-legged. Lately, she'd been adding aspects to her avatar—*for dramatic effect*, she claimed. Today she had chosen wind, which fluttered the cape she wore draped over a full suit of armor.

Barnabas looked up at Gar and grinned. "I think her costume is probably making this seem more serious than it is. It's just a friendly match."

Gar jabbed a finger at the two of them. "There is nothing friendly about you two when it comes to chess. You're both total lunatics about it." He lowered himself into a nearby seat with his water.

"I'm an AI," Shinigami declared. "I can't be a lunatic. I am inherently logical."

"That's demonstrably fallacious, and you know it." Barnabas moved a piece. "You justify every illogical thing you do by saying you *feel* like it. By that logic, all sentient life is inherently logical."

Shinigami stuck out her tongue at him and laughed at the look on his face. "Tabitha taught me that."

"Next thing we know, you're going to start carrying holographic sandwiches around." Barnabas looked mournful for a moment. "I miss the juice at Aebura's already."

Aebura's was a bar on High Tortuga, nestled away in one of the smaller cities. Barnabas had gotten hooked on the fruit juice she served when he'd helped the owner lead a slave revolt. When Tabitha had come to town, she had grown similarly partial—to the sandwiches. Now owned by Carter, a human, the bar was one of Barnabas' favorite hideouts.

Unfortunately, he'd done his job a little too well in Tethra. Everyone who might cause trouble was very, very dead, so he had no good reason to be there anymore. It was a great disappointment.

He shook his head to clear it and looked at Gar. "Keep training."

Gar grimaced, but he stood. Barnabas' voice was mild, but there was an unmistakable command in it. As a Luvendi, Gar had previously been too physically fragile to endure combat without fracturing multiple bones and dying. His time in the Pod-doc had made him stronger, both in muscle and in structure, but learning to fight was difficult for someone who had spent his whole life avoiding altercations.

In the past week or so, Gar had learned more about pain than he had ever hoped to know. He learned the feeling of muscle strain and strength conditioning. He now knew what his hearts felt like as they pumped blood faster and faster to circulate oxygen through his system.

He'd also learned about the bruises that came from slamming his fists—not to mention his knees, elbows, and feet—into a punching bag over and over.

Not to mention the fact that normal people might get a reprieve after a hard day's workout, but not Gar. The Pod-doc had also altered his body's various healing mechanisms so that he woke up each morning good as new—and ready, Barnabas pointed out, for more learning.

When Gar said that the learning was painful, Barnabas only said that pain was an excellent teacher, and provided the infuriating fact that the Pod-doc was capable of upgrading Gar to heal within minutes instead of hours.

"Why didn't you give me *that* upgrade?" Gar demanded, a bit desperately. He had a large bruise over one eye and was finding it difficult to see.

Barnabas blinked at him. "Pain is useful," he said again.

Gar privately swore that someday he would find a way to give Barnabas a bruise that wouldn't heal for a few hours. He'd bribe Shinigami to help him. He just needed to find something she wanted, first. Maybe a way of cheating at chess.

Unfortunately, it was difficult to be too angry at Barnabas, because the man pushed himself even harder than Gar did. He would strike the bag in a flurry of punches so fast Gar could not follow. The man always discussed the physics and efficacy of new techniques with Shinigami. They worked out new strike combinations, and Barnabas would train as though there were no end to his energy.

All this had impressed Gar, and that was *before* they had gone back to High Tortuga for a few days. During that time, Barnabas had sparred with a few of his colleagues from the former Etheric Empire. Gar had watched in awe, totally terrified. Potentially bone-crunching blows missed by mere fractions of an inch—or landed, and somehow didn't slow the combatants.

Even covered in bruises and blood, the humans seemed to enjoy brawling. Gar had decided that this was either inspiring or a sign of madness. He still hadn't figured out which.

He started his exercises again, taking care to follow form and not go too fast or over-extend. Barnabas had said time and again that form was the most important thing. Everything else flowed from that. Practice a strike incorrectly, and you could spend months un-learning poor habits.

Gar was already behind the curve. He didn't have time to unlearn anything. He barely had time to learn things in the first place.

"How close are we to—*ow*." His knuckles hit the bag wrong and skidded, leaving a trail of irritated skin. "How close are we to the syndicate's base?"

"Not far," Barnabas replied. He looked down at the chessboard and gave Shinigami a mock-angry look. Whatever move she had made—or whatever cheating strategy she had employed—had him rolling his eyes. "We're heading to Shu Base first to meet up with someone who might have the schematics. I want to make sure there will be no nasty surprises."

"*That's* why we're in the middle of nowhere," Gar exclaimed in understanding.

"You lived on High Tortuga," Barnabas remarked. "*That's* in the middle of nowhere. Shu Base is only *moderately* in the middle of nowhere."

Gar shook his head and went back to the punching bag. He was glad he was on the *Shinigami.* He would not want to fly out here all alone. A lot of people made their living as pirates, robbing the ships that passed through.

In the case of this ship, though, they would be biting off considerably more than they could chew.

Zinqued was exhausted. They'd drifted out here waiting for a mark to come along for the past three weeks, and so far, there had been a lot of nothing. In the first week, two cargo haulers had come by, but both had looked like they might be too well-guarded to be viable targets.

Now Zinqued thought maybe they should have gone for those.

He poured himself a cup of Stim-Drink. The stuff tasted terrible to a Hieto palate, but it did its job and would keep him awake for the three hours left on his shift.

He plodded back through the ship and up to the cockpit. He yawned and scratched at his scalp where the scales were more densely packed. Hieto had built-in armor over their torsos and somewhat tougher skin on their heads, which was both a blessing and a curse. They were hard to stab, for instance, but a lot of space suits and other technology didn't work as well.

Zinqued had barely sat down before the alarms started to wail. It had been weeks since they'd sounded. He startled so violently that most of the cup of scalding Stim-Drink hit him directly in the face.

He was still swearing and wiping it away with the sleeve of his coveralls when the rest of the crew bolted in to see what was going on.

"What kind of ship?" Chofal, their Yofu mechanic, asked as she tumbled in the door, swinging her head side to side excitedly. Yofu's eyes were on the sides of their heads, which made them ill-suited for anything that involved a standard screen interface, but their wide-angle vision and double-thumbed hands were fantastic for mechanical work. The engine room had never been in better repair than it was now.

"I don't know yet," Zinqued replied. He put the empty cup on the desk with a disgusted look. Now he was going to smell like Stim-Drink until he could wash his clothes again, and there was no telling when that would be.

What a day.

"It's probably just a—"

Chofal cut him off. "It's a small ship."

Zinqued groaned. The first excitement they'd seen in ages, and it was—

"A human ship," Chofal continued. She was definitely not the best person to be sitting in the copilot's chair, but she couldn't leave with everyone else crowded into the cockpit. She didn't look like she wanted to, either. Her head was cocked so she could read the information on the screen with one eye. "The...*Shinigami?*"

The rest of the crew shrugged, but Zinqued would have spilled the Stim-Drink if he'd still had any.

"The *Shinigami?* Are you sure? Are you *sure?*"

"That's what it says here." She frowned at him. "Why?"

"Because—" Zinqued flailed his hands excitedly.

Whenever they would stop to refuel, the other members of the crew would go through the shops and call their family members. Zinqued didn't care for trinkets and he had no family to call, so he tended to spend his time in bars.

And he had heard something *very* interesting the last time he was in one. Something very interesting, indeed.

There were a lot of people who stole ships for a living. Some even tried to turn it into a legal business on one end, re-registering the ships and sending them back onto the market, untraceable.

Rarely did Zinqued and his group bother with that. They were generally way out in the middle of nowhere. Who was going to come after them for stealing tiny ships? No one; not unless their victims wandered right into a Law Enforcement station and complained.

Even then, it was even odds that the police would be too lazy to do anything about it.

Like most people involved in the same business—legal or otherwise—they liked to trade stories, and even engage in some friendly rivalries. So when a captain named Klafk'tin had gotten rather spectacularly killed on Virtue Station, and his former first mate had started telling people *never* to mess with the *Shinigami*...

Well, word had spread. Especially when people found out what the *Shinigami* had on board—an incredibly powerful AI. You could sell one of those for more than you'd otherwise hope to make in a lifetime.

They'd heard the rumors of the captain, who was apparently terrifying, and knew a ship like that was bound to be armed. But no one was really worried about that. All ships had security, and any security measure could fail.

A friendly rivalry had been born. *Everyone* wanted to steal this ship now. Tik'ta's warnings had taken what would normally be a totally unremarkable event—just another ship stealer dead in the line of work—and had turned it into the biggest catch anyone had heard about in years.

Zinqued peered at the readouts popping up on his screen. Normally, he would say to let such a highly-armed ship go by. Better that than the chance they'd have to escape a trap and damage the equipment.

But this was the *Shinigami.* It was worth some risk.

Zinqued looked at the rest of them and grinned. "Warm up the net. We're gonna be legends."

2

The only sound in the gym was Gar drawing a breath like air was going out of style. The Luvendi lay spread-eagled on the floor and was staring at the ceiling with a glazed look.

Shinigami was examining a chessboard where her king was presently in checkmate.

"You have got to be *kidding* me," she said finally. Though her avatar's eyes weren't functional and she saw via the various cameras around the room, human mannerisms were getting more and more instinctive. She looked at Barnabas. "Did you cheat?"

"Look over your video logs," Barnabas suggested. "You'll find that every move is accounted for. No double moves, no moves where my hand went one place and the piece went somewhere else..." He shrugged elegantly.

Shinigami narrowed her eyes at him. "I noticed that lovely little speech didn't include the phrase, 'I didn't cheat.' You just mentioned a few specific *ways* you didn't cheat. You totally cheated."

"That's preposterous." He stood and retrieved his coat from where it lay on top of a set of weighted balls. He put it on and adjusted his cuffs. "You like to make a fuss, but we are roughly tied in how often we win."

"Only a human would call 52-48 roughly equivalent," Shinigami said in deep disgust.

"How many decimal points does it have to go before *you'd* call it roughly equivalent?"

"At least it should be within one percentage point!"

"Duly noted. We are *extremely* roughly equivalent, then."

Shinigami bit back a shriek of annoyance. Barnabas was incredibly adept at finding the subtle tells in *anyone's* behavior that indicated when they were annoyed by something…and then mercilessly exploiting that information to his advantage.

Barnabas glanced at the Luvendi. "Gar, how are you doing?"

Gar only whimpered in response.

"Mmm." Barnabas buttoned the suit jacket. "Well, I am going to go make myself a nice meal before we get to Shu Base. Somehow I don't think it will have very good food."

"Elitist," Shinigami uttered.

"I prefer to think I'm someone with taste buds. That's hardly—what was *that*?"

Everyone had looked toward the bridge when the proximity alert went off.

Shinigami's avatar vanished and Barnabas took off for the bridge. Left behind, Gar tried to sit up, moaned, and eventually settled for flopping onto his stomach and crawling over to the stack of mats to pull himself up. He tottered in the direction of the bridge, cursing his decision to get upgraded. His life before had been more dangerous, but significantly less painful.

He found Barnabas and Shinigami scrolling through information on the screen. They spoke so quickly that it took Gar a moment to understand the English. He could use his language implants, of course, but he enjoyed the process of learning languages.

Or, he *had* enjoyed it. Then he had discovered English, and learned a new meaning for the word "frustration." The language had clearly been created by a sadist. Gar had never heard any language in which it was so easy to communicate poorly.

"What's going on?" he asked. He tried to look casual as he went to his seat and sat down, but his legs gave out about halfway down and he ended up on the floor. He leaned against the chair and resigned himself to his fate.

Barnabas gave him a Look.

"This is my life now," Gar lamented with as much dignity as he could muster. "I hope you're happy."

Barnabas' lips twitched but he made no comment, for which Gar was grateful. "We're in a cloud of debris that shouldn't be here," he explained. "Our proximity alerts are going haywire."

Gar frowned. They had a fairly accurate set of maps that showed known asteroid belts and other hazards. An asteroid belt might be easy to navigate at normal speeds, but at high speed, a flight could come to a very quick and unpleasant end. This, though…

The ship swerved so quickly that the thrusters took time to recalibrate, and Barnabas looked up with a frown.

"Shinigami?"

"Working on it." Shinigami sounded annoyed. "Let me tell you, if you were human you wouldn't be able to deal with this. Even *I'm* hardly holding on."

"What kind of debris is it?" Gar asked.

"I don't know. Ship parts, it looks like. Some rocks." Barnabas frowned. "But that doesn't make any sense. I'll be back. I'm going to look out the windows."

Gar leaned his head back against the chair and waited as Barnabas' footsteps receded. The ship kept swerving and rolling, and he decided he was never going to be able to stand up again. That was all right. He'd had a good life. Maybe Barnabas would put an inscription on the chair in remembrance of him.

A few moments later, however, Barnabas' voice echoed through the ship in annoyance: "Son of a *bitch*."

Gar straightened up slightly. "Problem?"

"Not the one you'd think," Barnabas snapped, annoyed. "The debris field we're in? It doesn't exist. It's some artificial electronic noise made to make us *think* we're in danger, and…I don't even know."

"My guess," Shinigami voiced, " is that I'm supposed to take this very tempting and relatively debris-free path that's coming up."

Barnabas appeared back on the bridge. "I wonder where it leads."

"A trap!" Gar exclaimed. Did these people know nothing about how the universe worked? "It leads to a *trap*. We need to run away."

"Oh, Gar." Barnabas gave him a toothy smile. "Have you learned nothing about me by now?"

Gar groaned and dropped his head into his hands.

Zinqued watched breathlessly as the *Shinigami* wove its way through the artificial debris field. The pilot was truly extraordinary. Perhaps he could convince Paun to offer them a job. Zinqued's captain was a singularly joyless Hieto male, but he was a fair captain who neither blamed his crew for random chance nor stinted them on their shares.

He might see the value of a pilot that good. Then again, he might point out that taking on human crew members would be risky. Humans had a reputation, and a lot of aliens didn't like them.

Somewhat justifiably.

Zinqued looked back at the screens. Would the *Shinigami* take the bait? They'd moved closer to the "open path" he'd created in the artificial debris.

This had been one of his masterstrokes. Everyone knew all the old tricks—distress calls or blatant threats—when it came to stealing ships. They also knew those ploys were likely to backfire. Zinqued's first captain, a grizzled old Brakalon, had given Zinqued a priceless piece of advice.

"The trick is to get them to walk into the trap, thinking it's their idea," she had told Zinqued.

He'd never forgotten that, so he'd developed a new method—a series of signal-emitters that convinced the ship's sensors they'd flown into a debris field. It would be sudden, allowing them no time to think or react. The "debris" would get heavier and more difficult to fly through until, when all hope seemed lost, a relatively open corridor would appear in the field.

It was the sort of thing that might happen in a debris field, and ships fell for it every time. They'd alter their course and go straight for what they thought was relative safety...

Only to run right into the electronic net that overrode their systems.

Some people just vented ships at this point, but Paun had never been one of those. He would offer the captured crews the chance to ask for ransom from their family members, and even offer them a ride to a nearby station if they didn't make a fuss. He did put them in the brig, of course, but he'd always made a point of being fair.

He'd taken a lot of ships that way. People who might have stood and fought because they were sure they'd be killed would be so grateful they would give up the ship without complaint.

Zinqued's crew might not be the best-known ship thieves in the universe, but they generally made a tidy profit without much unnecessary risk. He liked that. They had a suite of tricks that allowed them to take bigger cargo haulers or small ships like this one. They could strike when the moment was right, and each collected a nice portion of the proceeds from each sale.

Now he watched as the *Shinigami* turned toward the nets. Zinqued was already planning the story in his head. He hadn't told his fellow thieves too much about his new trick, so he'd have to come up with some clever story as to how they'd captured the ship.

He sat back in his chair and started daydreaming.

There wasn't much to do at this point, anyway. The ship was as good as caught.

"There's something ahead," Shinigami reported.

Gar, who was in the process of hauling himself inelegantly into his seat, looked at the screens, overbalanced, and wound up back on the floor with a yelp.

"Would you like me to give you a hand?" Barnabas inquired. He leaned over the side of his chair, and could just see Gar's feet sticking out.

"No, that's fine." Gar gave a pathetic-sounding cough. "I like it here."

"I think you're really coming along very well," Barnabas complimented him. "Tomorrow's training session will—"

Gar whimpered. "No. I can't. I can't go through this again."

"Now, now. I'm sure if you—"

"I hate to interrupt," Shinigami began, a hint of danger in her tone, "but someone is trying to steal the ship, and I am trying to keep it un-stolen. Could we focus on that for a few minutes?"

"Ah, yes." Barnabas nodded at the screens. "I'm very sorry, Shinigami. Proceed."

Shinigami projected a set of infrared readouts. A strange device—slightly curved along one side—was emitting a signal. Barnabas frowned.

The sensors picked up more devices that formed a loose half-circle. Any ship that flew along this route, or even detoured slightly from the most common path, would find itself within range of the signal.

"Clever," Barnabas murmured. "If they'd made it a closed loop, you could fly around the whole thing—and most ships who even spotted it would try to fly under… and get caught in the second set of beams. What do they do?"

"They lock the ship in place," Shinigami reported. "Or, you know…that's what they do when they're functioning properly."

A spread of missiles streaked away, leaving the hull shuddering, and a few seconds later, each device disappeared in a flare of heat.

"I don't think they're working properly right now, though," Shinigami murmured innocently. "Not sure why."

"The universe may never know," Barnabas replied seriously. "Ah, well. A clever set of tricks, anyway. Is anyone uncloaking or moving to attack?"

"Nope. I doubt they would after *that* show."

"Mmm, good point. Well, onward to Shu Base, then. The sooner we get those schematics, the sooner we can take down Crallus." Barnabas peered around the edge of the chair. "Also, it looks like Gar could use a drink."

There was a muffled noise of agreement, and Shinigami laughed as she guided the ship in a smooth arc and headed toward Shu Base.

In the cockpit of the *Zumbir*, Paun's crew sat wide-eyed and slack-jawed.

"A whole missile spread!" Paun exclaimed finally. "I think it's safe to say we shouldn't go after that ship again."

Zinqued swung around. "Are you crazy? Do you know how much that ship is worth?"

"I've made my living by *not* going after ships like that, kid." Paun wasn't moved. "This is over."

But as he walked away, he missed the looks the crew sent one another. That ship was a freaking goldmine, and everyone knew it. Zinqued had the feeling that Paun was going to find himself overridden sooner rather than later.

They were *going* to get that ship.

3

The various sectors of occupied space had a few notable nuclei with a random assortment of star systems in between. It was difficult to identify any sort of *center* to things. After all, it seemed new races were coming out of the woodwork, and explorers from various species were finding new planets that were habitable, useful for resources, or both.

That said, if one were to identify the "fringes" of settled space, both High Tortuga and Shu Base would certainly qualify as being on them.

Shinigami used this as an opportunity to complain loudly about never being taken anyplace nice.

You're an AI, Barnabas retorted. He paced around a small shop on Shu Base while the owner sifted through various files. The shop was small and dusty—everything at Shu Base was dusty—with a selection of wares that ranged from schematics to, inexplicably, a caged animal that looked like a winged alligator.

Barnabas was giving that one a wide berth.

He placed his hand on the counter, then lifted it immediately, trying to conceal his look of distaste.

Oh God, it's sticky.

This is exactly the sort of thing I mean when I say you never take me anyplace nice.

You're on the ship. There would be no appreciable difference to you if we went somewhere nice.

I could at least look through your eyes. You know, catch glimpses of a universe forever beyond my grasp.

If this is a campaign to convince me to give you a body, you can forget it.

Damn.

Barnabas peered into the back of the shop. *I'm beginning to wonder if he's planning on assassinating me.*

One sec, hacking his systems. You know, we could just have done it this way.

That would be stealing. We have ample money, so there's no reason not to buy his goods.

You'd save so much time, though. No, he really is searching through the files. He's got the main schematics up—downloading those now—and he's searching through what appears to be various upgrades and weapons systems. I'm guessing he knows about some later modifications.

Well, that's heartening. I do prefer it when people don't try to kill me. How's Gar, by the way?

Practicing kung fu.

Barnabas pressed his lips together in a vain attempt to stifle his laugh. While aboard the *Shinigami*, Tabitha had watched a large number of kung fu movies, which she had left in the video banks in the room Gar now occupied.

While most humans would see the movies and laugh at

the corny dialogue and special-effect-laden fight scenes, Gar seemed genuinely inspired by the stories. Several times at meals, he'd waxed poetic about the stories of "honor and glory" he'd watched.

Barnabas and Shinigami had privately concluded that the Luvendi didn't have anything resembling movies. It was the only explanation.

The only problem, as far as Barnabas could tell, was that Gar really wanted to imitate the moves he saw. He did not seem to understand that the stories weren't *real* and the moves were useless in an actual fight.

They'd cross that bridge when they got to it, Barnabas decided.

The proprietor tottered back out with an oversized data chip.

"What did you say you were again?" it asked curiously. Barnabas honestly couldn't tell if it was male or female, and it seemed to be having the same trouble with him.

"A human," he repeated. "I am a male human."

"Human. Hmph." The proprietor seemed terminally unimpressed. Perhaps, in the grand tradition of merchants everywhere, it had decided that cash was the only equalizer it cared about. "Here you go, then."

"Thank you," Barnabas replied gravely. He slipped the data chip into his pocket and left before he could accidentally touch anything else.

Has anyone taken notice of the ship? he asked as he walked back.

If you mean with ill intention, then no, not that I can tell. The deck crew thought it was pretty interesting. It's probably the nicest ship they've seen in their lives, if I do say so myself.

At least you're not conceited. That's the important thing. Barnabas made his way up the gangway, nodding to the deck crew—Shinigami was right, they *were* staring—and entered the ship. *I think I need a shower before doing anything else. All of me feels sticky now.*

I mean...yeah, probably.

Half an hour later, in fresh clothes and with his hair still damp, Barnabas rapped on Gar's door. He heard a few kung-fu yells, then the sound of Gar running across the room to turn the movie off. The Luvendi appeared at the door, hastily stuffing a makeshift headband into his pocket.

Barnabas did not mention the headband. "We should discuss the syndicate plans if you have some time."

"Sure, yeah. Of course. What else would I... I mean, yeah. I'm free." Gar had enough sense to stop babbling, at least.

"So how is training?" Barnabas asked him as they walked. He couldn't resist having at least a *little* fun, after all.

"Oh, it's, ah...it's good. Yeah. It's going well."

"Better than a few days ago, then."

"Yeah." Gar's eyes lit up. "I realized what my problem was. I wasn't fighting *for* something, so I didn't have the mental fortitude to get through the pain. I needed to remember that I fight because I need to stand strong against evil. I need to be a force for honor and loyalty in the universe."

Is he for real? Shinigami asked in Barnabas' head.

I believe so. I'm trying to find it inspiring. After all, any of Bethany Anne's people would say the same if you asked how they persist through pain in her service. It's because they need to be strong to fight for good.

I guess. It's just so...so earnest. I want to slap him.

You don't have hands, thank goodness. Barnabas held open the door for Gar to precede him into the war room. *There are no print-outs?*

Nope. You have to get digital, Grandpa.

I object to every aspect of what you just said.

We ran out of paper.

That, I can work with. I'll get us more.

You're a very odd man.

Noted.

Barnabas brought up the schematics of the main base. "All right, this is the base that Yennai built for Crallus' predecessor when the syndicate joined up."

Gar stared at it with wide-eyes. "How the hell are we planning to get in there?"

"The normal way. We'll land, get off the ship—"

"And kill everyone." Shinigami continued. "Install a giant throne, and rule the world." Her avatar flickered into being, this time with a glimmering golden crown on her head.

"You and Gar are both really devoted to headwear," Barnabas observed.

"Says the ginger," Shinigami shot back.

Barnabas' hand came up to touch his hair self-consciously. Back on Earth, he had changed his appearance fairly frequently to avoid any inconvenient legends springing up.

It was a practice he'd started again. The year before he'd

changed his hair to a nondescript light brown. When they left High Tortuga, he'd begun making it slightly redder.

Perhaps he had overshot.

He noticed Gar staring at the definition of "ginger" in the dictionary. The Luvendi's face was a picture of consternation.

"It's a term for redheads," Barnabas explained. Gars' confusion only deepened, so he explained. "I have red hair now."

Gar's frown deepened even further. "No, you don't. Maybe some orange—"

"We're getting off-topic." Barnabas cleared his throat and tapped the schematics. "All right pay attention, all. *Here* are the landing bays. You'll notice that they are relatively far from the main base, connected by a series of trams controlled *by* the base, and easy to vent."

"So we dock somewhere else," Shinigami suggested at once.

"Well, yes. But where? It's hard to dock on the side of a base the way you would on a ship."

"Not necessarily." Shinigami began scrolling through the images. After a moment, she remembered to involve her avatar, who reached out to swipe at the images as if manually selecting and enlarging them.

She was getting eerily good at pretending to be human.

"Here," she said finally. She tapped one little hatch on the side.

"Is that the…garbage dump?" Barnabas asked. "Garbage chute?"

"It's always the garbage chute," Shinigami replied cryptically. *"Always.* It'll smell like ass, but it'll get you where you need to go."

"You know, I'm not even going to respond to that. How do we keep them from noticing us? Or shooting the ship as we set down?"

"Well, the space net incident gave me an idea. If we fly close enough, I can release some pucks with a signal transmitter attached. They'll hover near the base and convince the people watching the screens that there's a ship coming in to land at the bays. All the guns will swivel that way, and *we* will land elsewhere."

"You've only explained how to tell them there's something else there, not how to keep them from knowing *we're* there."

"We can move quite stealthily as long as we can take our time getting in there. Scanners rely on detecting various side effects of having a ship nearby. We'll cloak those and bibbidi-bobbidi-boo, there we are."

"Don't bother looking that up," Barnabas murmured to Gar. To Shinigami, he added, "This base is state of the art. For instance, if I remember correctly, the towers *here...* One second, let me enlarge this. Oh." He blinked in surprise. "You've tagged the relevant weapons and surveillance schematics into the main ones so that I can just tap on them."

"Yes. Paper can't do that."

"I see the point you're making, but let's move on." Barnabas frowned at the schematics on the table.

"Here's the other thing," Shinigami pointed out. "The garbage system is very close to what I believe is the main control center."

Barnabas chewed his lip. "There's a chance we're going to scare the crap out of some of the guards."

"Eh." Shinigami shrugged. "They work for a mercenary syndicate. Not like they think they're guarding people who go around giving out puppies and hugs for a living."

"I have to agree with her." Gar looked at Barnabas. "This base isn't usually inhabited. Anyone there came with the captains who chose to be here. We can't do much more for them."

"Crallus got in over his head," Barnabas murmured. "After everyone seemed to 'recognize' my Torcellan disguise last time, I did some digging. It turns out that Crallus now has some sort of second-in-command who might actually be running the show. He just waltzed in and took over, apparently. So whoever he is—"

"His name is Uleq," Shinigami informed him.

"'Uleq.' You're sure?"

"Who's Uleq?" Gar asked.

"We've run into him before," Barnabas replied darkly. "Killed his previous allies and ran off, and now he's representing the Yennai Corporation?"

"He was probably always associated with them," Shinigami surmised. "I'm guessing he took a brief detour to try something else and it blew up, and he took what he could and got out. He wasn't ever going to go down with the ship."

"He sounds wonderful."

"Doesn't he? So, do we have a plan?"

"Yes. Let's get in there and take Uleq out." Barnabas gave a grim smile. "Bethany Anne will be pleased, at least. Uleq. Sonofabitch! Well, two birds, I guess."

4

Crallus winced as he strode down the hallways of the base on Ur 5b. The Ur System was a particularly tumultuous one—a binary star system with a particularly noisy pair of stars. With the constant electronic noise from the stars, not to mention the heat that fried even mining equipment quickly, no race had bothered to settle here.

All the planets were gas giants, anyway. Conventional wisdom said that if anything managed to survive on those, it would make short work of all who tried to settle the place.

Ur's fifth planet, however, had a series of moons, one of which was almost constantly shrouded in shade. It was here that Yennai Corporation had built a hideout for Crallus' predecessor, and it was remote enough that Crallus had often found himself wondering where they had built *their* headquarters.

What was a step up from this? A base inside a black hole?

The Torcellan hurried ahead of him, hood up as always,

and called over his shoulder. "We don't have much time, you know."

"How can we not have much time?" Crallus was annoyed. "You said no one would find us here."

"I said it was extremely unlikely. I would *also* have said it was extremely unlikely that a single ship could take out several fleets of mercenary vessels." The Torcellan pushed his hood back slightly to make sure that Crallus could see the absolute contempt on his face. "Now, I suppose there's the possibility that all of your captains were entirely incompetent, as were the captains of Get'ruz Shipping, but I think it's *slightly* more likely that this is a dangerous adversary."

But only slightly, his tone clearly indicated. He kept up the pace as they hurried through the hallways.

"Since I do not wish to die here," he continued, "I will personally oversee the maintenance and review of our various defensive systems."

Crallus ground his teeth and tried to keep his silence, as he always did—but his temper was finally at a breaking point. They were being stalked by some creature out of a nightmare, after all. How much worse could it get if he pissed off the Torcellan?

"Why do you bother with us?" he snapped.

The Torcellan stopped and turned. "I beg your pardon?" His voice was icy.

"You hate us," Crallus continued. "You treat us like dirt, so why are you hiding here with the dirt instead of back at your big fancy Yennai base? Why are you bothering to have us be a part of your organization if you think we're so incompetent?"

His temper had been frayed to the breaking point for weeks now. He was tired, and he was in pain. First, he had lost three good ships on Devon, then Yennai had sent this Torcellan to keep tabs on him. He hadn't even bothered to tell Crallus his name. Next, Fedden had shot him in an attempted coup—making him paradoxically Crallus' favorite person in the syndicate, but the Torcellan had sent Fedden off to die for no good reason.

Hell, at least the kid had some balls. That was more than Crallus could say for some who had come with him. He was pretty sure they would lick his boots if he asked, which was ridiculous in a mercenary.

He didn't like the way they looked at the Torcellan, either—like maybe he held the power and they should switch allegiance. They might have already done so, for all he knew. Maybe it was just a matter of time until he was shot again and dumped into space.

In other words, he didn't particularly care what would happen if he voiced his questions.

The Torcellan, rather than becoming furious, appeared thoughtful as he studied Crallus.

"You question things," he stated finally. It was a simple observation, and it seemed to hold no rancor. "The others don't, but you do."

"The others didn't take over, either," Crallus rumbled. He lifted one shoulder in a shrug. "Some people like following orders."

"Yes," the Torcellan murmured. His reply was quick enough that Crallus could tell he'd had the same thought. "Yes, they do. But not you."

"No. Thing I liked about you lot was that you *weren't* sticking your nose into our business all the damned time."

"Why did you— Ah, yes. You took over from the last syndicate leader."

"Jillintor." Crallus could still remember the Brakalon, a weathered boulder of an alien who had been surprisingly easy to kill when all was said and done. Jillintor had lost his edge and led them into chaos. He had deserved to die.

However, Crallus was uncomfortably aware of the way things had been going recently. People might justifiably say the same about him. Fedden *had*, in fact. He and some of the captains had united and gone to face the *Shinigami* and its madman of a captain.

None had come back. Under normal circumstances, Crallus would have believed that would cure the rumbles of dissent for a while, but these *weren't* normal circumstances. He had a bunch of mercenaries holed up on a remote base with no alcohol, no enemies, and no women.

That was just a recipe for disaster.

Finally, the Torcellan ordered, "Follow me."

Crallus, who had been lost in thought, rushed to catch up, and he barely made it into one of the conference rooms before the door closed. An automatic lock clicked.

"I don't run the Yennai Corporation." The Torcellan folded his hands in his sleeves and began to pace around the table in the center of the room.

Unsure of what to do, Crallus stood awkwardly. He moved out of the way as the Torcellan circled the room.

"And?" Crallus asked finally when it seemed like the Torcellan wasn't going to say anything more.

The male shot him a sardonic smile. "I was considering

how to explain. I am the second child. My elder sister is a quick learner and a sycophant, and my father was eager to make her his heir. He never made any secret of the fact that he preferred her."

Crallus wanted to groan. This was nothing more than sibling rivalry, and he was caught in the middle. He wasn't sure where the human Barnabas fit, but he wouldn't be surprised to find that he had something to do with all of this.

The Torcellan's voice was like acid. "My sister, however, is blind to the true nature of the threats we face. Both she and my father think the humans are nothing to bother ourselves with. They say the universe has seen empires rise and fall, and nothing ever changes the fact that business prevails."

Crallus frowned. Then, wincing, he took a seat. He still wasn't recovered from the bullet wound Fedden had bestowed. His attempt at fancy manners was over.

"They don't understand the threat humans pose," the Torcellan continued. His voice carried the resentment of someone who has made a point time and again, only to be ignored. "They never give up and they never back down, even when it would be prudent to do so. They're damnably clever, they're ambitious, they have some bizarre sense of morals they think *everyone* should follow, and they fight like demons. If we don't stop them right now, they will spread over all of settled space, and we will have nothing left."

Crallus considered this. He wasn't used to thinking on such a scale. He had spent his life on various tiny ships, always aware of how small he was in comparison to the universe. He didn't mind that, though. It meant no one really cared about him when push came to shove. If he carved out his little slice, no one would stop him unless he really went out of his way to piss them off.

That strategy had worked out pretty well until now. He didn't want to think about the universe as a place waiting for one conqueror to come along and take everything, including the riches Crallus had accumulated over the years. They were his, dammit.

But he could see the wisdom of the Torcellan's words. The humans had taken over Yoll, they had defeated vast fleets, and then they had come to a tiny planet in the middle of nowhere and taken that over, too. And they were expending resources to keep it under their rule.

"We aren't going to win against the humans just by killing this one," he offered finally.

The Torcellan, oddly, seemed pleased. He took a seat and leaned forward. Crallus realized that simply by discussing this, he'd made himself a sort of ally. He wasn't sure how he felt about that. He still wasn't even sure how he felt about the Torcellan. Something told him this male was a snake, untrustworthy to the core.

"But if we can kill one..." the Torcellan continued. "Just *one*, and *most* importantly, get the ship with the AI core, we will have a chance. We'll have their passcodes, and we'll have computational power far beyond anything we could hope to buy now."

"Would you want to be their ally?" Crallus asked him. "They've allied themselves with other species."

"With *factions* of other species," the Torcellan snapped, "while the rest are forcibly silenced. No, the humans would turn on us in time. They wouldn't like most of what the Yennai Corporation is involved in." He gave a shrug and let out a sigh. "They might as well hate stars for the fact that light exists. There are always these types of industries, after all."

You said they could change that, Crallus wanted to remind him. He remembered the Torcellan's worry, and now he recognized the faint tension in his face.

The universe could change radically in the coming years, Crallus realized. Now that the Torcellan referred to the whole universe as if it were one cohesive object subject to massive forces, Crallus could see the truth of that. He couldn't see it any other way.

Humanity *might* change the whole universe.

Unless someone dealt with them.

"You came here because you wanted to prove to your father that you were right," he guessed.

To his surprise, the Torcellan laughed. He tipped his head back so that the hood fell from his shining white hair, and he laughed in a way that turned Crallus' bones to ice.

"I suppose I *could* tell him," the Torcellan admitted finally, "but I hadn't intended to. After all, once I have the *Shinigami*, Yennai Corporation really won't need my father at the helm, will it? Or my sister." His face was as cold and hard as the void outside. "I really don't care if they know I was right before they die."

5

Drakuz sat straight-backed in the sleek captain's chair on the bridge of the YCS *Jil* and tried not to look bored.

Because the truth was, this was boring as hell. He had been glad when his dedicated service to the syndicate had been recognized by Crallus. A ship as fast and well-armed as the *Jil* was something he could never have afforded on his own. Also, Crallus' favor meant Drakuz had fewer fees than the other captains, as well as his pick of the good jobs that came in.

Then, when the syndicate had withdrawn to the base on Ur 5b, Drakuz had been called in to fly patrols and protect Crallus. He had taken it seriously at the time. Doing this—establishing himself as the protector of the syndicate—might afford him an even cushier job flying patrols instead of going off on jobs.

Drakuz was a Shrillexian, so he *liked* fighting. But as you got older, all your old injuries seemed to multiply, and it got more and more difficult to keep up with the younger soldiers. A few years of flying patrols sounded like a nice reward for his service.

That was before he knew patrols could be so mind-numbingly boring. He contemplated stabbing himself in the eye with his knife, just to add some variety to the day.

"Something on the scanners, sir." Madrelub, one of the newer Hieto recruits, turned expectantly in his chair to Drakuz.

"Check it out, I guess." Debris. It was always debris. Madrelub frowned in consternation, and Drakuz remembered that he needed to act like a captain. "Old injury acting up," he muttered gruffly, rotating one shoulder. That excuse tended to get the respect of the younger soldiers, all of whom found the idea of being a grizzled old veteran to be exciting. Something to look forward to.

Drakuz had thought the same thing when he was younger. Now he knew that the grizzled old veteran with the war injuries was just bad-tempered due to pain.

Still, there was no convincing any young male of that. They'd have to learn it on their own. He gave Madrelub a purposeful nod, and the Hieto swiveled back around and began to run diagnostics.

"It's big," he reported. "Two hundred meters by—that can't be right. One moment, sir, running the diagnostics again. The distance keeps fluctuating."

The proximity alerts shrieked, and the helmsman swore. There were shouts as the *Jil* took evasive action and the ship's engines went into overdrive. The clamor only intensified when all of the screens went black and were replaced by an alien face.

It looked like a Torcellan, Drakuz thought. Pale,

anyway. But those eyes weren't quite Torcellan, and the hair *definitely* wasn't Torcellan, and the *teeth*—

This was a *human*, wasn't it?

"Hello," the face said. Its voice echoed out of every speaker simultaneously.

"Who… Who the fuck are you?" Drakuz hoped his voice came across angry, but he had a feeling all that came through was his fear.

"I am Shinigami." The voice echoed and slid through different pitches. The sound grated across Drakuz's skin, and he hunched his shoulders. It instinctively reminded him of what he'd imagined the monsters sounded like when he had been little and afraid of the dark. "*I am your worst nightmare.*"

"Call the base!" Drakuz barked at the communications officer.

"I'm trying, it isn't working!"

"Force the transmission through!"

The woman on the screen laughed. "Don't waste your time. I control all your systems." The image zoomed out until Drakuz could see her in the first mate's chair of her bridge. She raised one hand, thumb and forefinger pressed together. "Goodbye."

She snapped her fingers, and before their entire bridge went dark, they had just enough time to see that missiles had launched from her ship.

A moment later, the *Jil* was nothing more than debris.

"I really liked that," Shinigami remarked. "The snap added something to it, I think."

"Mmhmm." Barnabas barely looked up as he strapped slim-fitting armor in place over a black undershirt and leggings.

"And overriding their communications first worked well. I don't know how they saw us on their scanners, though."

"Mmhmm." Barnabas buckled the holsters into place and slid his pistols in carefully, smiling at their familiar weight. Knives went in the sheaths on his calves.

"And, of course, I got to see the type of transmissions they send for distress calls from Yennai ships, so we can use those if we need to later. Same encryption, same everything."

"Mmhmm."

"Also, I'm going to sit in the captain's chair."

Barnabas' head whipped around to stare at the nearest camera. "Don't you *dare*."

Shinigami projected an avatar that laughed and leaned against the wall. "Just wanted to make sure you were paying attention. You didn't say a damned thing about the scanners."

Barnabas gave her a Look.

"They shouldn't have been able to see us at all." She crossed her arms and shook her head. "I suppose I'm not surprised. It was only a matter of time until we ran into someone who scanned in a new way."

"At least it's just us and not the whole fleet in a pivotal battle," Barnabas said prosaically. He considered. "We'll want to find out how they *do* scan, though. And how they cloak. They must do both things differently than we do. Any information we can send back will be useful. Can we still run this mission, by the way?"

"We'll be fine. Gar's heading up, by the way. He looks good in his armor. You, meanwhile, look a little bit like a conquistador."

"Have you ever *seen* a conquistador?" Barnabas glanced at her wearily. "Because I have, and I look nothing like one."

"I'm just saying that your armor doesn't inspire confidence. Who'd rather be dressed in leather plating than badass plate armor? Bethany Anne's suit is *bangin'.*"

"You know, I spent centuries of my life without ever suspecting I would hear an AI use that phrase." Barnabas looked contemplatively into space. "It was a simpler time." He sighed. "And it's not like I'm actually wearing leather. It's entirely aesthetic."

"Says the ginger."

"I like this hair color! And *you* should be focusing on flying the ship."

"Mmhmm." She gave an eerily good impression of his interjection from a few moments earlier and projected dozens more avatars around the room. "Unlike a human, *I* can be in two places at once."

"Well, that's just unsettling." Barnabas gazed around.

All the avatars vanished, to the sound of Shinigami's laughter. "Mmhmm," Shinigami repeated, her voice echoing out of a nearby speaker.

"I'm here!" Gar jogged into the Pod bay.

"Oh, good. I—" Barnabas turned to him, and his eyebrows went up. They'd had the chance to secure some basic armor for Gar when he was last on High Tortuga, making use of some of the production facilities on the main continent. He hadn't told Gar about it at the time, since he didn't know how long it would be until he was comfortable having the Luvendi in combat.

Frankly, he wasn't sure he was comfortable with it now.

To be fair, Gar *did* look well-protected. His sparring recently had been impressive. He displayed good reflexes and a solid amount of force behind his strikes, given that he'd only started a few weeks ago. Still…

This is risky, Barnabas told Shinigami.

Yes, I know. You should go into the base alone.

You agree? Barnabas raised his eyebrows at one of the cameras.

Of course. You're a lone wolf. You do your best work alone. Only you can save the day.

You're mocking me, aren't you?

Barnabas, hero of the downtrodden, savior of the really bored crew on his ship.

I GET IT. Thank you.

He's going to have his first battle sometime.

Maybe not a whole base full of mercenaries, though.

You don't do small plans. It's going to be something *like this.*

Well played. Barnabas sighed and smiled at Gar. "How does the armor feel?"

"Heavy," Gar responded without hesitation "It's weird. I'm not tired of wearing it, but I feel like I should be because I never used to carry any heavy things. You know?"

"Sure." Barnabas nodded. "Now, you're clear on the plan?"

"'Let you go first," Gar confirmed. "I know. Believe me, I'm not going to go running off.'"

"Good." Barnabas swayed a little as the ship swerved. "Everything going well, Shinigami?"

"Oh, yes, just following in this ship's blind spot. I'm getting everything I can out of their systems. Oh, this is so good. They *still* haven't noticed me. One sec..." There was the shudder as a missile was released, and a moment later Shinigami laughed. "Yeah, they just never saw me at all. Pulled up, got all their information and their money, and now the ship is dust."

"Their *money*?" Barnabas asked.

"Well, sure. Under the maritime law—"

"We're not *under* maritime law." With a sigh, Barnabas turned back to Gar. "Now, remember to keep breathing. I think that applies to *your* physiology as well. The urge to start spraying bullets everywhere will be quite high. Don't do that. Keep breathing, pick small tasks like taking down one person, stay aware of your surroundings—"

Gar's eyes started to glaze over.

"And stay behind me," Barnabas concluded. "Battle is chaotic. There's really no way to understand that or prepare for it until you've seen it."

Gar now looked faintly queasy. "Maybe I should sit this one out."

"No," Barnabas replied firmly.

"Who am I kidding?" Gar looked around like a caged animal. "I'm a Luvendi. I started learning kung fu a month ago. Aren't you supposed to train for years?"

"In kung fu, yes. However, *you* have *guns*, and your aim is good. And your body has been enhanced. Also, what you've been learning has not been kung fu. Those movies aren't very…accurate."

Gar looked so crestfallen that Barnabas could have kicked himself.

I'm an asshole, aren't I?

You said it, not me. While you're at it, you should also tell him Santa isn't real.

Oh, God.

"The *themes* of the stories are realistic," Barnabas added hastily. "Honor and loyalty. The fight scenes are just, uh… stylized. Yeah. To highlight the, uh…greater themes of the, uh…metaphorical implications of the piece."

"Oh." Gar nodded. He looked a little confused.

I'm just going to hope he doesn't ask me to explain that.

You should have gone into academia or politics.

He isn't sad anymore, though.

You're really reaching, you know that?

The ship swerved again, and a few moments later, Shinigami's voice came over the speakers, sounding very pleased with herself. "That was the last of the patrol ships, and we're coming in for a landing now."

"And they haven't spotted us?"

"No. We're emitting the signal for the *Jil*. As far as they know, that ship is still patrolling."

"And what are they going to think when it docks at the garbage chute?"

"Way ahead of you, I turned those turrets off. None of the surveillance on this side is working. And, yes, the video feeds are being looped, so no one's going to notice."

Barnabas made a non-committal noise. In his experience, it was only so long until someone *did* notice, then all hell would break loose.

"As long as you're sure you'll be okay if they turn back on," was all he said, however. There was no need to scare Gar.

"Those piddly little things? Of course." She sounded offended that he'd even asked.

"Well, knock yourself out." Then, "This way, Gar. We're going to— Oh, my God, I'm going to be sick." As the door to the garbage dump opened, Barnabas pressed a hand over his mouth. "No one needs an upgraded sense of smell, I swear."

"We probably should have rigged gas masks," Shinigami remarked.

"Probably," Barnabas managed. "Ugh. Okay, let's get this over with before I think better of it all and let Shinigami use a nuke."

6

Gar and Barnabas crept over piles of garbage. Stations were generally built to minimize waste, so the massive bay wasn't even close to full.

It stunk to high heaven, however.

"This isn't so bad," Gar whispered to Barnabas.

"I wish I were dead," Barnabas grumped. He wore a look of resignation. "I don't know how I survived old Europe. This is a nightmare."

"It's only smells," Gar asserted. He wrinkled his flat nose at Barnabas.

"This from the Luvendi who threw a mug of tea across the room the other day."

"It was vile."

"It was *chamomile*. Who doesn't like chamomile?" Barnabas reached the door at the edge of the room and kicked a few pieces of unidentifiable detritus away from it. "At least we don't need to climb the garbage chute. That would be worse. Shinigami, do you have the codes?"

"Still working on it. Everything maintenance-related is on a much more secure server. I suppose that makes sense if I think about it. Sabotage must be a common way of destroying stations."

"It preserves the structure so that other people can just take over," Gar agreed. "Sometimes rival clans on Luvendan would do that—sabotage the air filtration systems or something and kill everyone in a tower, then fix the systems and take it for their own."

"No movies, no music, and everyone spends their time meditating unless they're busy committing mass murder." Barnabas snorted. "Remind me again why you left?"

Gar grinned at him. "All of us who leave ask ourselves that, and meanwhile, our families are writing to us, 'Come home! Why do you want to be out in the universe, anyway? Where could be better than Luvendan?'" He shook his head, wide-eyed. "*Everywhere.* The answer is 'everywhere.' Try convincing them of that, though."

Barnabas chuckled softly, then looked around when the door clicked.

"You're good to go," Shinigami told them. "It looks like you have four soldiers on their way right now. They'll probably directly intercept your path if you go straight, coming from the left two hallways above. And there are two more in the immediate vicinity. Not sure if they're patrolling or if they're actually maintenance workers."

"I guess we'll see." Barnabas eased the door open and slipped into the hallway, motioning for Gar to come after him. "Stay behind me," he whispered. "Let me handle this, and then once you've seen it happen, you can join in on the next one."

Gar nodded. He was suddenly drenched in sweat. Barnabas' description of combat had terrified him. He wasn't good with chaos; no Luvendi were. Chaos was just another chance to get injured.

There was a *reason* they spent so much time idle.

He clenched his hands into fists and followed, however. He could feel the new, stronger muscles moving below the skin. He was *not* too weak to move around in his armor. He was *not* too weak to strike with his hands and feet. He had guns, too, and he was good with them. Barnabas had said he had a natural talent.

He could do this.

What kept him here, however, wasn't his belief in himself. It was his shame that he might leave Barnabas to do this alone. Gar could not expect his allies to go into danger while he sat on the ship in relative comfort and safety. That would be wrong.

Ahead of him, Barnabas walked quickly and lightly down the hallway. A few paces from the turnoff point Shinigami had indicated he held a hand up to stop Gar. Shinigami had been correct. The soldiers were coming toward them, and the way they clanked as they moved told Barnabas that they were in fact soldiers.

"Like I know how to fix an intake valve," one of them was complaining. "I *don't*. We should have brought actual mechanics with us."

"We had to run quickly," one of the others countered.

"Yeah, that doesn't sit right either. We fight people who come after us, right? We're soldiers, but we're just turning tail and running? I don't like that. Anyway, what's the use of a base if no one knows how to use it? You panic and run, and when you get out here you realize no one brought mechanics? That should be part of the plan."

Barnabas nodded to himself. This seemed like a sensible complaint.

In agreement or not, he launched himself around the corner with his knives drawn. Someone devoted to fighting their way out of things, especially someone who was already frustrated about being cooped up here, was not going to walk away from this whole thing without a fight.

He reminded himself of Shinigami's words: *there's no saving everyone.*

These mercenaries had shown that they gladly supported slave traders, and Barnabas knew they'd kill him without a second thought. He owed them nothing.

He caught the first in the throat with his knives and the mercenary, a Torcellan female, went over backward with wide, surprised eyes.

No guns. He didn't want anyone to know they were here yet, and it was hard to hide the sound of a Jean Dukes Special.

One of the others, perhaps the complainer, raised his weapon to fire, more out of instinct than anything else. His jaw hung open.

He never got the chance to squeeze the trigger. Barnabas' hand shot out, and he wrenched the gun away. The mercenary stumbled forward as Barnabas bent the barrel of the rifle and proceeded to club the male over the head. The male went down in a heap.

One of the remaining two drew in his breath to yell for

help, and Barnabas crushed his throat. He was a Hieto, which meant that the throat had thick skin that would have resisted most combatants.

Barnabas, however, was not "most combatants." The Hieto fell with a wheeze and went still, and Barnabas turned to the last mercenary with a grave look.

"You knew this would be your end," he stated simply, having read the female Torcellan's thoughts. She had gone to her friend, who now lay dead on the floor. Both had enjoyed a life that would make decent people shudder—killing, stealing, enslaving.

They had called it 'the good life,' and they had told each other that they were probably going to die young.

Barnabas met her eyes and felt a sense of calm come over him. Some deaths were unjustified.

Hers had been earned.

"I judge you," he declared and drove the knife into her eye. She fell without a sound.

Gar, who had been watching, stood behind Barnabas with his mouth open. There had been some chaos, yes, but all of it had been contained within Barnabas. To the naked eye, what had occurred here had taken place in a mere few seconds.

Gar was still staring in shock when he heard Shinigami's warning through his implant.

"The other two are behind you!"

It was too late. There was the click of a gun, and Gar spun to see a Shrillexian with his gun pointed directly at Gar's head.

With his gun up, the Shrillexian started to laugh. He

lowered the weapon and elbowed his patrol partner in the side, still laughing.

"A Luvendi in armor! Have you ever seen anything so ridiculous?"

Barnabas walked up next to Gar. "You see what he's doing here? Lowering the weapon, laughing, talking with his compatriots? Never do that."

Gar didn't even glance at Barnabas. His chest rose and fell faster now, and he could hear the steady beat of blood in his ears. "Shut up," he ground out.

Barnabas fell silent and his eyebrows shot up in surprise, but then he realized Gar wasn't talking to him. The Shrillexian, meanwhile, laughed even harder. His companion, a Brakalon, began to chuckle as well. He swung his big head from side to side in mirth.

"A Luvendi in armor. Heh heh, that's a good joke."

"I said, shut *up*," Gar snarled.

"He wants us to shut up!" The Shrillexian fought for breath. "He might spit on us if we don't!"

He was still laughing when Gar's hand closed around his throat. Gar dragged him close with a hiss, and the Shrillexian's face met Gar's other fist—hard. The punch shattered the front of the Shillexian's skull, and the laughter trailed off in a gurgle.

Whoa, Shinigami exclaimed in Barnabas' head.

"Whoa" is right. Don't worry, I'll take the Brakalon if I need to. Gar might—WHOA.

Gar launched himself at the Brakalon and lashed out with nearly surgical precision. His hands and feet found joints, internal organs, and painful pressure points. The Brakalon howled as he doubled over, clutching his face, and Gar brought a knee up with lethal speed to bash into his skull.

The Brakalon collapsed, and his chest no longer moved.

Gar turned to Barnabas with wide eyes and a dawning smile on his face. "That felt *great*," the Luvendi exclaimed. He was heaving for air, but his voice was full of satisfaction. "All those years of them thinking they were better than me because they could fight and I couldn't. Well, now I can."

Is it possible we made a mistake? Barnabas asked Shinigami privately.

Hellllll no. *We made a great choice. This is going to be fantastic.*

So, definitely a mistake, then.

Barnabas nodded. "That was well done. Good job going for the Brakalon before he stopped laughing."

"Yeah!" Gar looked around. "Where's the next group? I want to do that again!"

Shinigami, see if you can find some data on manic traits in Luvendi. Barnabas held up a hand in caution. "Stay on point," he advised. "When you start seeking out fights to have fun, you get blinded to the true purpose of fighting, which is to achieve an external goal."

"Oh." Gar looked a bit ashamed. "Right. Uh…right." But his eyes scanned the area as if he might find some other enemies lurking. "Well, let's go clear out this base and find Crallus and Uleq."

"Good focus. Check your weapons, make sure everything's still secure. Good? Come on, then. They're up two flights of stairs from here, and at the back of the base from where we landed."

They headed off, Gar still bouncing on the balls of his feet.

He felt like he was walking on air. The feeling he had gotten when his strikes landed had been exhilarating, and the fact that he had been able to win a fight with speed and training was something he was sure would *never* get old.

And he was actually helping! He loved that. Before, when Barnabas completed any number of missions, Gar'd had to wait on the *Shinigami*, feeling miserable and useless. He couldn't pilot, he couldn't pull information up nearly as fast as Shinigami could, and he hadn't been able to fight —until now.

For the first time, he really felt like he was part of the team.

He hummed happily to himself as he walked. He wasn't sure what the tune was; maybe one of the songs that played during the movies he'd seen. He'd begun to appreciate music these days. Maybe other species were onto something with that.

He just felt incredibly benevolent toward the whole universe right now.

He was still humming when they came to what the schematics said was the stairwell, and instead discovered a post-construction addition to the base. The stairwell was a good twenty yards away, and between them and it...

There must have been two dozen mercenaries, all with their weapons slung across their backs or leaning back in their chairs. They were playing cards and laughing with one another, and they turned toward the door as it opened.

A human and a Luvendi. It was clear from a single glance that Barnabas and Gar didn't belong.

Barnabas had his gun out and was firing even as one of the mercenaries ran for the alarm button. The shot blew him backward, but not before he'd punched the thing. The alarms wailed.

"Damn," Barnabas said succinctly.

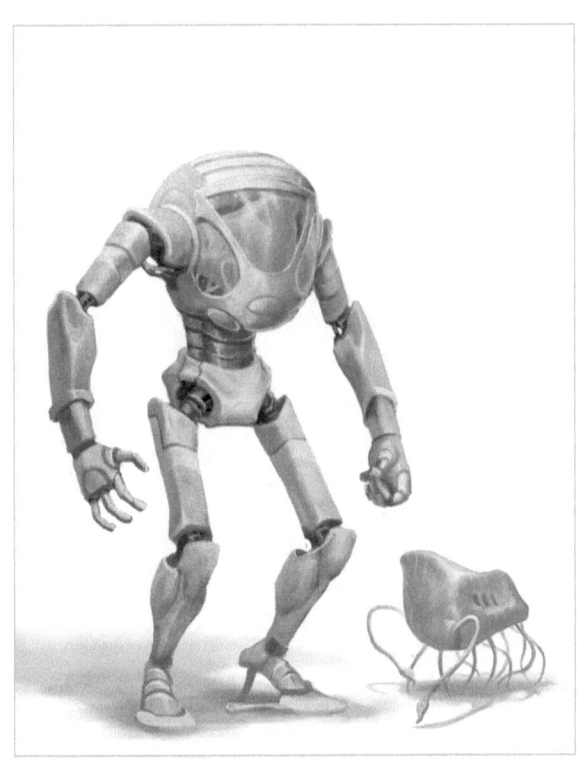

Jotun image by Eric Quigley

7

The alarms blared to life, and Tafa looked anxiously at the door. "What do you think that is?"

"Clearly," Jeltor intoned, "we're under attack."

Tafa gave him an unfriendly look. She and Jeltor were the only two surviving members of a raid on a passenger ship. The mercenary captain, a Shrillexian named Drakuz, had graciously offered to enslave them rather than leaving them to die in the wreckage.

Actually, he'd told them they could be mercenaries if they wanted to. Then he'd laughed himself sick.

Tafa hated him.

She *knew* she was scrawny. She didn't need it pointed out. She was an artist, not a laborer. She was Yofu, and it wasn't like the Yofu made very good soldiers. She had sometimes wondered if that was why her cousin's family was so involved in the munitions business—they wanted to take soldiers' money since they couldn't be soldiers themselves.

Tafa had thought that was a stupid idea, but now they were billionaires, and she was a slave on a mercenary base. Maybe there *was* something to doing things their way.

Jeltor, a Jotun male, looked down on everyone else and liked to make a big deal of how nice his power suit was. He was also, Tafa had learned, incredibly vain. Insulting his appearance was one of the few ways she could get back at him when he was snide.

It wasn't even difficult to do. Jotuns were purple blobs with wavy arms and two very bulbous eyes. Jeltor's body looked like a clump of jelly that was about to burst and spill every which way. For all she knew he was a supermodel by Jotun standards, but he was prickly enough about it that she couldn't resist sliding in little insults.

"You'll have to be careful," she said innocently. "You wouldn't want the stress and fighting to ruin your looks."

His power-suited chest wheezed as he looked at her, then stomped off to the corner to sulk.

Tafa sneered at him, but her heart was pounding far too fast. Someone was attacking the base.

What if they just assumed everyone here was part of the syndicate and killed them?

"What's going on?" Uleq strode into the rooms with his silvery hair still sopping wet and plastered to his neck.

Crallus didn't mention that. Torcellans were notoriously vain about their hair, and this particular Torcellan was notoriously fond of murder. Crallus wasn't going to die because he'd looked at someone's hair the wrong way.

He brought up the video feeds from the lowest level. "The alert was pressed here, on the maintenance level. Two patrols are down, and they are presently fighting in the recreation room. I've blockaded the doors up to the first and second levels and have reinforcements stationed at intervals."

Uleq cast an annoyed glance at the screen, where two figures wreaked havoc in a room full of mercenaries.

"How did they get *in?*"

"I don't know yet." Crallus shook his head. "But that seems to be all of them, and I have the ones on the second level readying rocket launchers." He hesitated. "I've written off the ones on the maintenance level."

There wasn't any evidence in Uleq expression to suggest he cared in any way who lived or died. He brought up the second set of surveillance cameras on the outside of the station and drummed his fingers impatiently on the desk while he waited.

Both males could see immediately what had happened. The *Shinigami,* not the *Jil,* was attached securely to the garbage dump at the end of the base.

The Torcellan slammed his fingers down repeatedly on the keys, sending commands to the gun turrets.

"Why aren't they firing?" he snarled.

Crallus only shook his head. He didn't know, but he had a very bad feeling about this. Barnabas clearly knew not only where the base was, but he also knew its layout. He'd avoided the traps at the main launchpad, and he must have found some way to shut off the security feeds and the defense systems.

He was still trying to figure out what to do when Uleq

grabbed a communications device Crallus hadn't seen before. "Captains to your ships," he ordered curtly. "There is a ship docked at the end of the base. Keep it pinned down." He switched off the device and jerked his head at Crallus. "Come with me."

"Where are we going?" Crallus followed him out into the hallway, turning his head briefly as he heard an animal yell and the sound of something breaking.

Uleq gave him a look. "Where do you think? We're leaving. They must have gotten into the servers at the other base." He cursed, low and fluently, in his own language. "There's no way they've found the main Yennai base, though, so that's where we're going."

"If we go back without the ship—" Crallus began nervously.

Uleq cut him off with a bitter laugh. "We don't need to worry. My father and sister will be glad to see me fail. They like to gloat. They'll give me orders, then forget about me again while they keep trying to turn themselves into Torcellan royalty." His lip curled. "And then they'll be dead," he whispered to himself.

"Update," Shinigami reported to Barnabas and Gar. "Uleq has sent a fuck-ton of ships to pin me down."

"How many exactly is a fuck-ton?" Barnabas brought the butt of his pistol down on a mercenary's head and nodded in satisfaction as the soldier dropped like a stone. To be fair, the soldiers hadn't run, but they also weren't very good at this.

As far as Barnabas could tell, they mostly showed up at their targets and overran their enemies in a large group. Most of their enemies would be at about the same skill level, and the rest would run.

They had no Plan B.

Unfortunate for them, but not really his problem. He was just the messenger, so to speak. And his message was that they were terrible at their jobs and were consequently going to die.

"There are eighteen of them,: Shinigami explained. "So not really a fuck-ton, just enough to be annoying."

"Only you would say that about eighteen ships." Barnabas took a moment to watch Gar clothesline a mercenary with a rifle and snickered slightly before he came back to the topic at hand. "Ah, right. Fuck-ton of ships. Can you get out of there? We can hold on here."

"They're trying to override the holds I placed on the system. Right now I'm in a dead zone regarding the turrets. They never anticipated needing to shoot at their garbage compactor apparently, which seems like an oversight. But the point is, as soon as I lift off I'll have eighteen ships and all the turrets to deal with."

"Hmm." Barnabas spun, unsheathed his knives, and charged into the middle of a group of mercenaries who were massing to take Gar down. They dropped one by one, screaming.

"Don't worry about me. I'm trying to get the turrets back online, so I can take the ships out with their own weapons. I always did like poetic deaths."

"Mmm. Be careful, and tell me if you need help."

"I appreciate the sentiment, but you're still relatively

squishy and don't take missiles to the face well. You handle the mercenaries, I'll handle the ships."

"Good call." Barnabas took down the last assailant on his side. Gar had three opponents left, all with their weapons drawn.

"You take the one on the far left!" Barnabas flipped up both Jean Dukes Specials and took out the other two with simultaneous shots. Gar's gun went off a scant half-second later.

He looked at Barnabas with a grimace. "You took out a lot more than me."

"Practice," Barnabas replied. "You'll get there."

"Uh-huh," Gar agreed glumly. Barnabas started laughing, and the Luvendi got a prickly look on his face. "What? What's so funny?"

"It's just, uh..." Barnabas bit his lip. "You look like something out of a horror movie. You're *covered* in blood."

"I was fighting," Gar argued. He frowned at Barnabas. "Why are you *not* covered in blood?"

"*Where* you stab people is important," Barnabas pointed out.

"Fuck!" Shinigami's voice echoed through both Barnabas and Gar's implants.

"Problem?" Barnabas' hand went to his pistols.

"They're lifting off! I'm guessing it's Uleq, and there's no way I'm going to be able to reach them. I'm trying to turn the turrets on, but by the time I get them pointed at the ship, they're going to be gone." The rough snarl of her voice sounded supremely frustrated. "I've launched pucks, but there's something in their cloaking signal that's confusing the little buggers. I figure their own turrets might have a better chance, but—"

"Focus on getting a trace on that ship," Barnabas instructed. "We can find them wherever they go. We can get wherever they go. Don't worry."

"I'm not worrying. I'm an AI. It's literally—"

"Impossible for you to be illogical, yes. You've mentioned. I'm just, uh...reassuring Gar." Barnabas shook his head confidentially at Gar, who stifled his laughter. They would just have to hope that Shinigami was too busy fighting off mercenary ships to look through their eyes.

"Oh. Right." As Barnabas had expected, she didn't bother to check up on them. "Yeah, it's going to be okay, Gar."

"Thank you," Gar replied solemnly. He hadn't gotten the hang of speaking through the throat mic yet, so his reply was audible.

"And all of this gives me an idea," Barnabas murmured. "Come with me."

He climbed the stairs two at a time and opened the door slightly to peek out. He slammed it shut and jumped to the side the next moment as several bullets pierced it.

"Yep, that's what I thought. Shinigami, can you get me into their intercom systems? Bonus if it can be broadcast to the ships as well."

Fight off a fleet, Shinigami. Trace the ship, Shinigami. Get me into their intercom systems, Shinigami. Wash the dishes, Shinigami. Her mental voice clearly reflected her disgust.

There's a dishwasher on board, and that doesn't count as you washing the dishes.

Hmph. Nevertheless, she added, *you're good to go on the intercoms. I'll just route your words through me. Doing all the heavy lifting. Again. As usual.*

Barnabas ignored her.

"Attention, mercenaries of Crallus' syndicate. Crallus has ordered you to fight us. Meanwhile, he has left the base with Uleq. We can go about the rest of this one of two ways. Either you lay down your weapons and meet me on peaceful terms, or we'll kill all of you. I would prefer not to massacre you all, but as the bodies of your friends downstairs will show, I won't stand by while people shoot at me. End broadcast."

There was a pause.

"Twelve of the ships have stopped shooting," Shinigami reported. "I'm trying to get into their security feeds to see what's going on. Oh, yep. They feel betrayed."

"They're not wrong to," Barnabas pointed out. "Can you do something for me? Yes, before you say anything, I know. Another thing for Shinigami to do. You're so overworked. But this time you get to make things blow up."

"I'm listening."

"Make an example of the ships that didn't stop shooting at you."

"Oh, hell yeah. One sec. Yep. Yep, that's the good shit. Just look at those beauties."

Gar frowned in consternation.

"I'll bet you thought you were missing *quality* conversations before you had the implant," Barnabas remarked.

Gar snorted with laughter.

"Let's see how you behave when *you* get missile launchers. Oh, yeah. Gorgeous. Lots of explosions. I'll play the holo for you when you get back. Do you want to let the rest leave?"

"One moment. Broadcast my voice again."

"Okay, you're good to go."

"Members of Crallus' syndicate." Barnabas kept his mental tone light and pleasant. "At the conclusion of my last message, twelve ships stopped firing on the *Shinigami* and six continued. Those six ships are now debris, and their crews are dead. The other twelve are still floating. I trust the implications of this are clear. For those of you who want to survive today, I have the following instructions: all twelve ships will land, and all mercenaries who want to survive will go to the landing bays. The captains will come to see me, and I will explain my terms. Any ship that lifts off will be shot down. Any mercenaries who fight will be killed. I will meet you in Crallus' office in half an hour. End broadcast."

"That's a tight timeline," Shinigami commented.

"Good. Make it tight enough, and they'll focus on that instead of making trouble."

"You'd be a diabolical parent. I'm just saying."

"Having met Alexis and Gabriel, I am quite content with my life as it is."

"We'll see. By the way, the mercenaries are clearing out, except for a handful, and I'm reading two life signs in an out-of-the-way room with locked doors."

Barnabas' eyes narrowed. "I'm going to go check that out. Come on, Gar." He pushed the door open, directed five shots at the mercenaries who reached for their guns, and strode through the hallways, shaking his head.

"Why is it that the ones who want to fight are always the stupid ones?" he asked conversationally.

Gar had no answer.

At the locked room, Barnabas paused and looked over his shoulder in amusement as the captains yelled for people to get out of the way, they needed to get to Crallus' office.

They're panicking, he commented to Shinigami.

Couldn't have happened to a nicer group of people, I tell you. They scratched my paint. Make them pay.

Will do. Barnabas opened the door and stared at the two occupants. One appeared to be a jellyfish wearing a robotic suit, and the other was a Yofu. She held her hands high and looked completely terrified by Gar's blood-drenched form.

"Don't shoot!" she begged. "We're captives! I'm Tafa Boreir, and this is—"

"*Boreir?*" Barnabas asked delicately. "As in, a relation of Mustafee Boreir?"

"He hates me, and the feeling's mutual," Tafa replied at once.

A quick scan of her mind showed only hatred for Mustafee, but Barnabas wasn't willing to trust her yet. This would require more in-depth questioning, and he did not yet have time for that.

"You'd better hope you're not lying," he told her. "Because I killed him about a week ago, and I've been dismantling the Boreir Group ever since." He looked the two of them over and noticed the restraints on both the robotic suit and the Yofu's neck. She also had bruises, and marks where there had been manacles.

"You two will accompany me to Crallus' office," Barnabas announced. "We'll see what they have to say about your presence, and I'll decide what to do from there."

8

The captains stood in awkward silence as Barnabas sat behind the desk, Gar at one shoulder and the two prisoners off to one side.

The captains no doubt thought that Barnabas sat in silence as a power move. In reality, he was reading their minds one by one. He saw greed. He saw apathy. And more than once, he saw families with children.

If it had been all the captains, Barnabas knew he would have seen more anger and blind rage. These, however, were the ones who acknowledged Crallus' betrayal. They were willing to see reason when faced with a force stronger than them.

He closed his eyes slightly and tried to focus on all of them and none of them at once.

"Here are my conditions." His voice was not loud, but there was no compromise in it. "When you leave this place, you leave behind all ties to this syndicate and to the Yennai Corporation. Any equipment and any weapons Crallus has given you will be left here.

"You are released from any debt of honor to your fallen comrades, beginning with Jutkelon and the others who came to Devon. They chose to support slavery and the murder of innocents. You lose no honor by refusing to take up their fight. Let it be.

"You may continue as mercenaries, but you may not protect those whose business was forbidden by the edicts of the former Etheric Empire. In the future, you will be bound by the laws of the Federation, and you will use your best efforts to avoid all dealings that are not only illegal but also immoral.

"Do not go back to Devon. Do not *speak* of Devon. From this day forth, if anyone asks you about the planet, you will claim to know nothing. Do you understand?"

He looked at each of them and felt their cautious acceptance.

Mostly. One of them, at the end of the line, was already thinking of revenge against Barnabas. He planned to tell everyone he met about Devon.

"You may think that I will not know if you violate the terms of this agreement," Barnabas continued. He did not look at that captain specifically. "But I assure you that I will. And I *will* find you, and you *will* pay. Today I am giving you a chance to redeem yourselves. Do you understand?"

They nodded. They understood. Even the captain at the end of the line *understood*. Barnabas stood and went around the desk to stand in front of him.

"Your first thought was to tell everyone about Devon as a means of revenge," he observed. He smiled at the look on the alien's face. "Oh, yes, I know that. You were smart enough not to keep fighting when you were clearly outmatched, but you never had any intentions of meeting my demands, did you?"

The other captains looked on in silence, and the Shrillexian drew his lips back in a snarl.

"You are prey, and you will die as prey."

Barnabas laughed before he could stop himself. "I see."

"A predator doesn't *talk*. A predator doesn't make demands. A predator kills. And if you aren't a predator, you're prey." The Shrillexian gave Barnabas a cold smile.

Then he gave a gasp as Barnabas' hand closed around his throat and Barnabas forced his thoughts into the alien's head.

I am no one's prey. I am a Vigilante. I offer redemption to those who have the potential to seek it. His eyes glowed red as he stared the alien down. You *do not.*

The Shrillexian fell to the floor, dead, and Barnabas returned to his chair. He looked at the other captains and felt their fear. It was the fear of those who had followed bad leaders, who had believed that the innocent might be punished for the mistakes of the guilty.

"I knew that he intended to lie to me," Barnabas verified. "I know as well that the rest of you intend to meet my demands. There will come a time when it will be easier to take the well-paying job and not ask a question. There will be a time when you are tempted to tell people what you know of Devon. Do not. *I will know.*"

The captains nodded, terrified.

"You will go now, and you will take the mercenaries who are in the landing bays with you."

More nods.

"One more thing," Barnabas said. "These two prisoners. Who are they? Don't speak," he told the two of them.

"Drakuz picked them up," one of the captains offered. He cleared his throat. "He took their ship, and they were the survivors. He hadn't decided what to do with 'em yet when he got called to the base, so he just brought 'em with him."

"I see." Barnabas looked around at the captains. "You may all go. Leave this place, and never return to it."

They almost ran, they were so eager to be gone, and Barnabas turned to the two prisoners.

He studied them, testing the surface of their thoughts. The one in the robotic suit—a Jotun, Shinigami had told him—had thoughts that even *felt* like jello, though Barnabas wondered if that was just his mind tricking him based on the creature's appearance.

It was smart, though. He would have to remember that. Its mind was buzzing with schematics and plans, however strangely those thoughts might manifest.

Tafa Boreir was a problem. More accurately, she was a question. The more time she had to be alone with her thoughts, the more Barnabas saw images flashing through them—strange landscapes, stylized portraits, abstract splashes of color so vivid that he almost got the sense of music from them.

Still, he could think of any number of reasons she might hate Mustafee, and having an artist's soul didn't mean she was incapable of cruelty.

Not by a long shot.

He would have to question her further at some point, but for now, she was injured with nowhere to go. His course of action was clear—he would take both Tafa and the Jotun onto the ship, heal them, and determine their allegiances.

If they were truly innocents who had simply been in the wrong place at the wrong time, he would let them off at a safe station or base with enough funds to get back to where they wanted to be.

If they weren't...

That wasn't something he needed to think about just yet. Why waste time worrying about the future before the facts were known?

Barnabas stood and nodded to them and Gar. "We should go." *Shinigami, is there anywhere else you can dock while the mercenaries are leaving?*

There's a docking port that leads directly out of Crallus' office. Pretty clever, though you'd have to be desperate to use it as an escape. I'll put down there. Gives me a better angle to keep an eye on the other ships anyway.

A few minutes later, Barnabas led the two former captives to the med bay. The Jotun simply needed maintenance on its suit, which Barnabas would attend to later with Shinigami's help. He led Tafa to the Pod-doc, however.

"If you lie down in here, we will fix your injuries and disable the control device implanted in your brain."

She gave him a look that was far too shrewd for comfort. "What if I'm your enemy? You didn't seem sure before."

"I'm still not sure," Barnabas told her. "But I'm not the sort of person who weakens my enemies with control devices and imprisons them."

"What sort of person are you, then?" she challenged him.

Barnabas didn't blink, though he sensed that her mind was suddenly flooded with images of torture. The methods were very inventive and had the weight of old memories, not just imagination. She had seen these things done to people.

If she was part of Mustafee Boreir's family, he wasn't surprised.

"If you are dangerous enough that I would need to take such measures," he said gravely, "I will simply kill you."

This seemed to reassure her, and she nodded. "I'd prefer that."

"You've thought about this before." It wasn't a question. Barnabas stared down at her in the Pod-doc and read that she had decided this at a very young age.

"My aunt had my parents punished when I was young," Tafa told him. The images that accompanied this memory were brutally clear in Barnabas' mind. "They weren't executed until a few years ago, though."

"You miss them."

She turned her head directly toward him, and he realized that for a Yofu, that was the equivalent of a human looking away. With her eyes on the side of her head, she could not see him when her face was pointed right at him.

"I don't think about them," she told him by rote. Her thoughts had closed off entirely. "I don't really remember them. I just know I don't want to die like they did."

Barnabas had the suspicion that Tafa had become an artist to make herself unworthy of notice. She had worked hard to make sure she was not a threat to Mustafee, and she had also spent a great deal of energy not thinking about the parents she couldn't save.

To his surprise, he felt a lump in his throat. Catherine's decline had been relatively quick, but if he had been forced to live for years or decades knowing that she was in pain every day—

The wave of black across his mind was sudden and strong. He swallowed and fought his way back from it. He would *not* go back to that place.

"I do not indulge in cruelty for its own sake," he stated, both to Tafa and the Jotun. "There are crimes for which I would judge you, but I would never do so without cause. Rest. We will heal you, and then we will determine what to do next. You will not be a captive or a slave no matter what happens."

He left before his thoughts could get the better of him.

9

"It has to be Virtue Station. It's risky, but we can't stay on this ship. We have to change over as soon as possible." Uleq slouched in his seat, feet up on the desk in front of him. Since he no longer needed his hood, he had taken the time to dress his hair and done whatever else it was that Torcellans did with their appearances. Crallus wasn't sure. He just knew he didn't think much of it.

He didn't even grunt a response.

"You object?" Uleq asked almost delicately. Crallus could hear the latent order in the male's voice. *If you're going to object to my suggestion, you had better have a good one of your own.*

Like Crallus gave a damn. He grunted this time and looked away, shaking his head. *Please let this conversation be over.*

Uleq didn't take the hint. His boots thudded on the floor of the bridge, and he leaned forward, narrowing his eyes. "Is something wrong?" he asked dangerously.

"We left them to die," Crallus burst out finally.

The Torcellan stared at him incredulously for a long moment. His expression said that he could not even imagine someone being upset about this.

"Of course, we left them," he agreed finally. "The human was going to kill all of them regardless. We managed to save ourselves, but we could not possibly have saved the others—not with the humans in our systems. The only reason we got out at all was that this ship can be piloted manually. If it couldn't be..."

Crallus said nothing.

The Torcellan's frown deepened. "You closed all the doors and left the ones on the maintenance level to die."

"That was different," Crallus argued. Guilt twisted his gut, but he pressed his point. "I did it because they couldn't be saved, but the others might have been."

"Precisely. We did the same thing when we left." The Torcellan looked smug, as if this were the point he'd been making all along.

"It's. Different." Crallus ground the words out. "I did what I did to save as many of my syndicate as I could. To protect the *group*. What *you* did admits that there *is* no group. That's a failure. A leader who fails like that isn't a leader anymore. If that many of their soldiers die..."

He didn't finish the sentence, but he couldn't escape it in his own head. *Then they deserve to die too.*

He could tell himself that he hadn't really known Uleq intended to leave without the mercenaries. It was even true...sort of. It wasn't like Uleq had explained the plan. He hadn't mentioned the mercenaries at all. It was conceivable that he might have had a plan to get the soldiers out, especially when he took them to the second and cunningly hidden set of trams, which couldn't be vented to the outside.

He had known what sort of person Uleq was. It had been abundantly clear that Uleq cared only about himself. He had wanted the mercenaries because he believed they could help him capture the *Shinigami* and take control of the Yennai Corporation. Otherwise, they were expendable.

Presumably, he felt the same about Crallus. He had probably kept Crallus around half because he couldn't outrun him on the way to the ship, and half because he thought Crallus would help him find a new group of mercenaries.

Like hell, Crallus would do that.

"Those mercenaries were not just pieces on a game board," he said angrily. "They were *my responsibility*. Some of them were my friends." At least, they had been so before he took over the syndicate. No one was really a *friend* after that. It was a side effect he hadn't considered—that they would become potential challengers.

Still, he hadn't wanted to throw them away for no good reason. He had tried to protect them, no matter what Fedden had said.

The Torcellan looked at him so blankly that Crallus wanted to laugh. It was almost funny. It really was. The concept of mercenaries as friends—as *people*—was so far outside Uleq's thought processes that Crallus' words didn't even make sense to him.

The Torcellan really *had* just thrown all of them away as

a failed gambit; a learning experience that he would account for in his next plan.

It made Crallus want to strangle him.

Then Uleq gave that small, superior smile Crallus had always hated. "*You* left them to die, too," the Torcellan told him with a shrug. "I don't see why you're complaining. You left to save your own skin."

He turned to the instrument panel with the air of someone who had won a moral victory and Crallus stared at him, his breath coming in short gasps.

He hated Uleq. He hated him more than anything.

But he was right.

Barnabas bounced on the balls of his feet as he waited for Gar to attack. After the battle at the syndicate's base, Gar had showcased a similarity between human and Luvendi physiology: he had fallen asleep so suddenly that he hadn't even made it out of the shower.

Shinigami had turned the water off, dimmed the lights, and declared there wasn't much more she could do. Barnabas, she suggested, could bring a pillow.

Barnabas had disagreed with this assessment.

After a good few hours of sleep—enough to fix the subsequent crash after the adrenaline from the fight—Gar had appeared sleepily in the main part of the ship, rubbing a crick in his neck. Barnabas was certain that if he'd had any hair, it would be sticking up straight on one side. The Luvendi inhaled about three times what he usually ate, and passed out again on his plate.

This time, Barnabas *did* bring him a pillow.

There wasn't any particular rush, after all. They were trailing the unnamed ship that held Crallus and Uleq, having caught up with it after the base had fallen.

Shinigami had rigged the facility to display a warning message to anyone who tried to land there or take it over, leaving Barnabas to contemplate what to do with it. It wasn't a very useful location for farming, but perhaps a factory?

Something to decide later. For now, since Gar was finally back upright, Barnabas would focus on sparring.

Gar rushed him, surprisingly quick on his feet, and Barnabas nodded approvingly as he rolled out of the way. They circled for a few more seconds before Gar rushed again. Again, Barnabas slid out of the way, and Gar looked around, surprised that his adversary had disappeared.

The third time Barnabas did it Gar growled, "Why won't you fight? We were supposed to fight!"

Barnabas said nothing, but a little smile played on his lips as he waited.

He was not going to attack. It was important that Gar learn about frustration. Right now, Gar felt invincible and wanted to use his new physical strength to solve every problem. He needed a reminder to use the skills he'd spent a lifetime learning before his enhancements.

If he was going to be a part of Barnabas' team, he needed to learn to fight with his mind as well as his newfound strength. There would inevitably come a time when the odds arrayed against him were so great that he would walk into a trap if he didn't plan things carefully.

Gar believed he lost to Barnabas because he didn't have

as much strength and speed, or as much experience. While true, this concealed another truth: he wasn't planning his fights at all.

As Gar darted at Barnabas again, Shinigami reported, "They're making plans to dock at Virtue Station. As far as I can tell, they don't know we're behind them. It could be a ploy, but I don't think it is."

Barnabas rolled out of the way of Gar's charge, but he felt fingertips brush him as the Luvendi went past. Gar, knowing that Barnabas tended to go sideways, had grabbed for him. Barnabas nodded at his opponent as he came to his feet and returned to his circling.

"Good," he told Gar. "I think you're right," he added to Shinigami and Gar. He'd added in the distraction of mental discussion during the sparring sessions.

After all, it would be a part of Gar's experience in combat.

The next time Gar charged, Barnabas saw him look for some clue as to whether Barnabas would go left or right. Barnabas tapped his sternum as he moved. "Watch the core," he told Gar. "That's where all movement begins. Even strikes."

Gar might be tired and new to this, but he was willing to learn. He charged again, and this time he managed to follow Barnabas as the man jagged left.

Unfortunately, he forgot to think past catching Barnabas, and so caught a punch to his chest. Gar's eyes went wide and he wheezed as he doubled over, hands still clutching Barnabas' shirt.

Barnabas allowed him no respite. He hauled Gar

upright and punched him in the face. One strike after another, he drove the Luvendi back across the floor.

"You were winded," he told Gar brutally, "but the fight doesn't stop when you get injured." Another strike, but this time he grabbed one of the Luvendi's long arms and flipped him onto his back. The distribution of weight was similar enough to a human that the same techniques worked, although a Luvendi's shoulders were set up differently. "If you stop the fight when you get hit, your enemies will take the opening, and they will kill you. Also, since you got your breath back a few seconds ago, you have no reason not to be fighting back right now."

Gar struggled up and landed one weak punch. He made one last half-hearted effort and charged at Barnabas with a battle cry.

Barnabas didn't hesitate. He slid smoothly out of the way and let Gar face-plant into the wall. The Luvendi slid down, looking somewhat dazed. Barnabas noticed the Jotun and the Yofu standing in the doorway, staring slack-jawed at the scene in front of them.

"He'll be fine," Barnabas assured them.

Gar moaned slightly from the floor, though whether it was in agreement or disagreement, Barnabas couldn't say.

Well, I suppose this is as good a time as any to ask the Yofu more questions. Keep an eye on Gar, would you?

What am I now, a nurse?

I hope not. God help your patients.

I'll have you know I have an encyclopedic knowledge of human physiology and diseases and the computing power to accurately diagnose problems in seconds that would take human doctors weeks.

Mmm, and you've never once done that, have you?

Of course not. I have more important matters to attend to. But I'll keep an eye on Gar for you.

Thank you. Barnabas wiped his face with a towel and headed out. Time to learn all he could about Tafa.

10

Barnabas saw the Jotun lurking as he came into the hall, and that gave him a sudden idea.

The Jotun species clearly thought they were superior to all other alien races, taking great pride in their intellect. If Barnabas were to question this one—Jeltor, was it?—the alien would be insufferable and take great joy in talking circles around Barnabas. He had already gotten the sense that it masked its true thoughts by concentrating on inconsequential things while he was around.

That meant he had to catch it off-guard.

And he was fairly sure he had a good angle—using its obvious condescension to Tafa against it. When he came out of the gym, he spoke brusquely to her.

"I'd like to speak to you about your cousin." He gave her a brief, hard look and waved negligently down the hall as he strode away. "I'm going to clean up. Wait for me in the second conference room. The ship will give you directions."

The ship? *Rude.*

I'd rather they didn't know everything about you yet.

Oh. That makes sense.

Mmm. Barnabas gave a respectful nod to the Jotun as he passed. He took his time changing, and offered a silent apology to Tafa; he'd explain all of this when he spoke to her. Then he wandered back out into the hall with a glass of water in his hand and his hair still somewhat wet.

The Jotun, as he had hoped, was still lurking.

He's trying to get into my systems, Shinigami reported. *I'm not sure it's malicious, per se. It's his way of learning about us. I'm feeding him false information, though. I don't think he's caught on.*

Barnabas tried not to grin evilly. *Good. See what you can get from him in the meantime.*

Oh, I am. Their suits are actually very impressive. I'll be selling this to Jean for sure.

Giving. *You'll be giving it to Jean.*

Oh, come on! She'd be thrilled to get her hands on this.

Yes, of course—piss off the woman who makes our weapons. That's going to go well. Because if she fails to kill us herself, you know she's going to bring John in.

Oh.

Yes.

Barnabas gave the Jotun a brief nod, then frowned as if he'd had suddenly had a thought. "Did she speak to you about her family?"

"I knew who they were, of course." Jeltor could have made a career out of sounding artfully bored. "Impossible to ignore *that* last name. But she never spoke about them, no."

"I'm getting that sense." Barnabas shook his head in mock annoyance and sighed. "I should have known better than to hope for any useful information out of one of them. What's weird is, I'd done some digging and I didn't come up with any mention of her parents."

As he'd hoped, Jeltor was eager to display his superior research skills. "You wouldn't. They were the family embarrassment."

Barnabas, already walking away, looked back as if this information was unexpected and interesting enough to detain him. He leaned closer. "Really? How did you ever find that?"

"I have my sources." Jeltor was as smug as the cat that got the cream. The suit didn't provide any facial expressions and the jelly-blob body was as unreadable as ever, but Barnabas was *sure* the thing was smiling. He seemed to weigh the pros and cons of talking, and the pros won out. He shuffled a few mechanical steps closer. "They joined a group of troublemakers. A little terrorist group called the *Hyo-Tein*."

Translation?

Fuck if I know. It's not coming through. Unless it's a mix of Brakalon and Leath, in which case it means "Umbrella Fart."

Barnabas pressed his lips together in an attempt not to laugh. *I, uh...I think that's unlikely.*

Be careful, though. Her voice was suddenly grave. *Be sure he's telling you the truth, and if he is, tread lightly. I'm coming up with nothing about these people, which means—*

Boreir Group wiped them off the map.

Exactly. And you cut the head off the snake, but we still haven't gotten some of their executives yet.

Noted. To Jeltor, he said, "I've never heard of the *Hyo-Tein.*"

"You wouldn't have," the alien assured him confidently. "They haven't been around for decades at this point, because of *her* parents. Not that they wanted the group destroyed, no. But Boreir Group was… Hmm, let's say they were *particularly* harsh because members of their family were involved. They're the ones who got it classified as a terrorist group after they killed everyone. If you find stories about them, they'll be the stories Boreir Group planted."

This was interesting. Barnabas leaned against the wall, arms crossed, and nodded for Jeltor to continue. Two things were clear: the alien was telling him the truth, and he enjoyed knowing things no one else knew.

"Her mother's parents were clerics," the Jotun explained. "So I guess she had some ideas in her head about how the universe should work—and of course, then she fell in love with one of Mustafee Boreir's brothers. Now, Gedden Boreir—that's her father, you know. Yes?—wasn't ever going to inherit. It was always Anafee, and her son after her. So I'll bet he thought he could just do anything he wanted. Maybe he wanted to mess with his sister a bit. So he joins this group, and they start lobbying to disallow the sale of munitions to a few of the larger planets."

Barnabas started to feel a bit uncomfortable. He had a fairly good idea of what was coming—or at least the general idea—and it was not good.

"He probably thought he was going to get a talking to." Jeltor tried to make it a joke, but he failed. "They didn't bother. His mother told Mustafee to take care of it. It was a test; her first big test for her heir. Let's just say he passed with flying colors."

Barnabas felt a low throb of anger. "But they kept Tafa alive?"

"Of course. She was just a child. They're not *monsters*, after all." Jeltor's voice dripped with sarcasm, and Barnabas could feel his genuine disgust at what had happened. For just a moment, Barnabas saw a thought flash through the Jotun's head—a family with children and siblings, many generations. There was love there, and a deep horror that anyone could hurt their family the way Mustafee Boreir had. Jeltor paused, then admitted, "I suppose I don't blame her for being…how she is."

Barnabas thought back to Tafa—earnest and defiant, cloaking her feelings in black humor and resolutely shoving away thoughts of her family. She had chosen to be a painter. What did that say? What did it say that she still tried to make something beautiful, even after her early experiences?

He was not sure. He nodded to Jeltor, however. "Well, thank you. I never would have guessed."

Jeltor gave a stiff mechanical nod. He seemed embarrassed to have shared a moment of genuine emotion with Barnabas.

As Barnabas walked away, he considered. That bit of conversation had been more successful than he had hoped, and he had a better, not to mention more reassuring, picture of Jeltor's character.

Tafa's story, however, was horrifying.

She was sitting straight-backed in her chair when Barnabas entered, thoughts resolutely blank. She was terrified of what was coming.

"I'm sorry I was delayed," Barnabas told her. He slid into the chair opposite her. "I'm sorry I was curt with you before, as well. I have a lot on my mind."

It wasn't the explanation he wanted to give, but it would have to do.

Tafa looked at him mistrustfully, so Barnabas decided to come at this from a direction she wouldn't expect. "Your paintings are beautiful."

She froze, her eyes widening. "How…"

"Your thoughts," Barnabas admitted. "You know I can see them, yes? I told you all as much when we were with the captains."

"I didn't think you really *meant* it." She sounded horrified. "You saw my— I never show *anyone* my paintings!"

"No? You should. They're very good."

"You can't even see them the way they're meant to be seen." She wasn't trying to be insulting. "You look at things with both eyes at once. *My* paintings are for Yofu."

Barnabas considered this, his eyes distant. He thought back to the images he had seen. Yes, they had always come in pairs, meant to be seen simultaneously. That was fascinating.

"You know, I was once a monk," he told her. "In human history, before we had the technology to print words, we would copy out our knowledge by hand. Monks—a sort of religious figure—would write the books out very carefully, and they would make art in them. There would be drawings on the page, and they would make the letters beautiful. We called them 'illuminated manuscripts.' To make them was a sort of religious devotion; service to God. I got the same feeling from your paintings." He hesitated, then added, "I know you didn't mean to show them to me, and I'm sorry I looked without your permission."

"Most aliens can't read minds," Tafa murmured finally. She didn't say anything about her paintings, though Barnabas had felt a flare of grief when he described them as religious. Knowing her history, he wondered if he had been closer to the mark than he had guessed. "I mean, I know Ubuara kind of can, but they can't read *other* species' minds."

"Most humans can't," Barnabas agreed. "I'm a rather unique case." He decided not to share the details. He would rather not touch off a firestorm by explaining just how he had come to be modified.

Tafa hesitated. "If you don't mind, I'd rather skip all the pleasantries. What do you want from me? What are you going to *do* with me?"

Barnabas sat back in his chair. "I wanted to make sure you weren't another Mustafee," he told her bluntly. "I wanted to make sure you weren't doing the sorts of things he did. I'm now quite sure you're not. I understand why you wouldn't work against him. I suppose the question is, what do you want to do with your life now that everyone in your family who wanted to hurt you is gone?"

She looked at him with a storm of emotion in her eyes. She'd never considered a universe like that; never dreamed that it might exist. Images flashed through her thoughts one after another—seeing new planets, new people. Painting. Learning languages.

Then reality returned, or what she thought was reality. Gray and depressing, it filled her thoughts with the reminder that her family's money had been the only thing that stood between her and starvation. With them gone, she believed she had nothing.

"Stay here." The offer came easily. "Until you decide, you can stay here if you want. You're not obligated to do so."

She gave him a wry smile. "I have no skills other than painting."

"Then we'll get you some paints," Barnabas replied. "Take any of the suites. It doesn't matter which."

"But I can't... I don't..." She frowned as he stood up. "Look, I'm the family disgrace. They only kept me around as a warning to the rest of clan. I'm of no use to you."

Barnabas gave a small smile. "You don't have to be."

"Why not? Why would you give me something if I'm not useful? Why would you keep me alive?"

Barnabas paused. "Because the measure of a person isn't how *useful* they are," he said finally. "With me, people don't earn their lives, they earn their *deaths*. You've spent your whole life trying to be nothing, but you found beauty even in that. What could you do if you weren't always looking over your shoulder? I think you should get a chance to answer that question."

Shocked into silence, she said nothing, and he left her to sit in peace. He was halfway to the kitchen before he looked at a camera, frowning at Shinigami's unusual silence.

What, no mockery about the sappy speech?

No. Her answer was immediate. She said nothing more, however. In the unexpected silence, he sipped his tea and thought about Tafa's paintings and Gar's redemption, Jeltor's family, and Crallus' mercenaries as the *Shinigami* burned toward Virtue Station.

11

"I don't know, Zinqued." Chofal sighed. She stared at the device he'd put on the table between them. "I don't think this is a good idea."

"What, because Paun said not to keep going for the ship?" Zinqued snorted. "Paun just doesn't want to play in the big leagues."

"There's something to that," Chofal said seriously. "You know how those rivalries are, people are getting killed all the time when you get to that level."

"Yeah, but the ones who don't die, get rich! *Really* rich." Zinqued nodded meaningfully. "You have *no idea* how rich, Chofal."

"What do I need money for? I've got a good life."

"Really?" Zinqued gave her a look. "You're totally fine living in a tiny bunk, eating freeze-dried food and drinking Stim-Drink for the rest of your life?" He sensed he had her, and since he knew what Chofal wanted out of life, he gave the last little push. "You could have a big mansion on your home planet. A huge workshop, too, full of spaceship parts.

You could have your own dock full of ships and just tinker around with them."

She gave him a wide-eyed look. Clearly, she'd never thought about this. Still, she wasn't sure. "You *saw* the kind of weapons that ship had," she argued. "We don't have those—and I don't think anything I do will make us fast enough to outrun them."

Zinqued patted the device on the table. "That's why we use this, right? It can burrow in and inject a virus into their computer systems. It'll shut everything down, they won't have a chance in hell of defeating programming *this* sophisticated." He'd paid through the nose and called in every favor he had at their last stop, but it would be worth it. "I just need you to make sure it can latch on securely and get through the hull."

Chofal wavered, but as Zinqued had guessed, she was too proud of her work to resist. She had a healthy appreciation for the other ship...which meant she wanted to get her hands on it. The idea of using her engineering skill to knock out the computer systems she didn't understand—and thus feared—was just too tempting.

She nodded and snatched at the device.

"I'll do it," she said with a grin. She swung her head from side to side to see him with both eyes, a bit nervous but also excited by the challenge. "It'll be ready in a couple of days."

"A day," Zinqued corrected. "Who knows when we'll come across them again?"

"What are you talking about?" Paun's voice suddenly cut through the air, and Zinqued looked up to see the captain looking between the two of them, his eyes far too knowing for comfort.

Chofal rescued the situation with some quick thinking. "Zinqued had an idea for a new device to help us steal ships." She told the half-truth with simple sincerity. She hoisted the device up to show Paun. "I told him I'd have it done in a few days, but he reminded me it's been a while since we've seen a likely ship, so we need to be ready when we do see one." She pushed herself up and nodded. "I'll get to work on this. Engines are running fine, nothing much else for me to do."

Paun gave a long look at Zinqued when she was gone, and Zinqued tried to look as innocent as he could. Finally, Paun sighed.

"Let's hope this device of yours works," he said shortly. "Easy marks are getting fewer and farther between these days."

Zinqued stared after him in surprise as he left. He'd thought they would have to follow the *Shinigami* against orders, but with Paun getting more and more worried about finding another haul...

Yes. It was quite possible that Zinqued could get the captain to agree to this scheme.

He grinned as he made his way to the ship's tiny kitchen. *We're gonna be legends.*

They made good time to Virtue Station in the tiny name-less ship. Crallus spent most of it checking the sensors obsessively, but nothing ever showed up on the scopes.

Was it possible that the *Shinigami* hadn't noticed them leaving? That it had guessed their port wrong and was racing to find them in another direction? He'd been sure that they would look behind them and see that damned human, but none of his fears had come true yet.

By the time they docked—Uleq's family money had eased the way, and the Station Manager practically fell over himself to welcome them—Crallus had begun to think all of this had turned around. No matter how he felt about the mercenaries he'd left behind, it was hard not to feel a rush of relief at their sudden safety.

Which was why, when they found their change of ship blocked, Crallus didn't at first understand what he'd heard.

"I'm very sorry, sir." The Station Manager practically cried as Uleq stared him down. He was wringing his hands. "Mr. Jodu says that on the orders of Ilia Yennai, you must meet with him before the ship can be released."

Uleq's face went stormy, and Crallus guessed that Ilia must be his sister.

For a moment, he felt amused at the plight of the station manager. It was bad luck to be caught between the high-ranking officials of a company as large as the Yennai Corporation. But it'd be a good story for him to tell later.

Then Crallus remembered that to Ilia, Uleq was the rebellious younger brother who'd probably lost the family significant money as he feuded with Barnabas and the former Etheric Empire.

And Crallus was certain to be caught in whatever trap Ilia set for her brother. He gave a heartfelt inner curse as he hurried after Uleq, who was striding upstairs to the main level with murder writ plain on his face.

"Uleq—"

"It will be *fine*," Uleq ground out. He looked over, and to Crallus' surprise, he could see the history of this rivalry as clear as day. Uleq had always been the younger, inexperienced sibling, never the favorite. He had tried to be clever, to earn his father's respect, but nothing had worked—all the glory went to Ilia. Now she was determined to make him pay for what she viewed as a poor choice while she continued blindly on with a course of action Uleq knew would be ruinous.

He was furious, and Crallus could hardly blame him for it.

Then the walls came down behind Uleq's eyes, and there was only the alien who had told Crallus that his father and sister would die without ever knowing why. The one who had sent Fedden on a suicide mission because executions stirred up bad sentiment. The one who had sent Crallus' mercenaries to die so that Uleq could escape.

This Torcellan was dangerous. Crallus put his head down and followed, regretting all the choices that had led him here. Could he slip away? Would that be possible?

He still hadn't thought of a way to do so as they entered the bar that housed the station's largest bank—a part of the Yennai Corporation, as it happened. Everything here was Yennai, except for the vendors that were so small as to be insignificant. Crallus would bet that even they traded information, though.

Mr. Jodu turned out to be a Brakalon, which took Crallus aback somewhat. Brakalons made excellent guards. They were difficult to kill, strong as steel, and practically impossible to frighten.

They weren't usually bankers. He'd never seen one in a suit before.

Jodu stood and ducked his large head in a nod. "Mr. Yennai. I—"

Uleq slammed something onto the table, and the guards had their guns out in an instant. But Crallus stared at the thing with his jaw hanging open. It looked like a bar of pure etreusium, which would make it…

Close to priceless.

"Will *this* be enough?" Uleq's voice was dangerous, and everyone in the room heard the threat. Uleq might be unarmed. He might be here due to the wishes of a more powerful member of the Yennai Corporation.

But his voice said that if Jodu didn't take the deal, Ilia's protection wouldn't arrive before Uleq's retribution.

Fortunately for everyone, Jodu was a sensible Brakalon, and Uleq had chosen his offer well. Untraceable and worth millions on the open market, the Etreusium was enough of a bribe for anyone to disappear.

Jodu slipped it into the pocket of his coat with a smile. "I will tell your sister that I believe your return to the Yennai Corporation will cause no undue problems."

"Do that." Uleq snarled, and he pushed his way back out of the room with Crallus at his heels.

"Please, let us offer you refreshment while the ship is readied." Jodu must have brass balls, Crallus thought, to engage with Uleq again. Far safer just to let him leave. But the Brakalon didn't flinch as Uleq looked back at him. "It will be only a few minutes, but space travel is so uncivilized. A nice meal, perhaps?"

Uleq paused, and Crallus prayed.

Then Uleq nodded. He allowed himself to be shown to a table and sat in silence as food and drinks were brought and the servers melted away. Then he looked at Crallus and said simply,

"I'm going to enjoy watching them die."

1 2

"I hate stations." Jeltor sounded pained as he looked around at the interior of Virtue Station. "It's always the very worst sorts that try to take shelter in places like this. And no matter what they do with the decor, one can never forget how unnatural it is to be making a permanent home in space."

Tafa thought this was more than a bit ridiculous, given the fact that the Jotun couldn't leave their home planet's seas without their robotic power suits, but she didn't mention that.

"Are you coming, or aren't you?" She braced a hand on one hip.

"I'll come," Jeltor confirmed, with the put-upon tone of someone who is only doing a favor for a friend. *But I won't like it,* his voice indicated.

Tafa was in too good of a mood to care. She set off at a quick pace—well, for her short legs—and climbed four levels from the glitz and soft music of the banks. Barnabas had transferred money into an account she could access and told her to buy whatever she wished for the next few weeks on the ship. He'd advised her that if for some reason the *Shinigami* had to leave suddenly, she should find lodging and he would pay for it when he returned.

Why he would have to leave suddenly…he hadn't said.

Tafa planned to get clothes and toiletries—her one set of clothing needed to be washed. She'd looked like a child playing dress-up in human clothes the last time she washed hers. Plus, human toothbrushes just did not work in Yofu mouths, and there were a few things even the *Shinigami* couldn't synthesize.

But first, she wanted to look at art supplies.

She'd done her research, and she knew there was a shop on this level that had paints and brushes. It was quieter up here. The first couple of levels on either side of the main banking level had to do with Yennai Corporation business in all its forms: parts, information, mercenaries, money. The rest of the station was only tangentially related.

She liked this level. Someone was playing the flute, and the hallways were clearer. Shopkeepers chatted with one another and were sharing tea, and a few called out greetings. Jeltor seemed to take this as a personal insult, but Tafa only smiled and shook her head at him.

Her family was dead. This should trouble her, but all she felt was relief. Her parents should have died long ago, before their years of torment—and after that ordeal, death was a mercy. She mourned their passing and welcomed it in equal measure.

And Mustafee had deserved to die. When Tafa asked, the ship confirmed that Barnabas was hunting down the remaining members of the Boreir Group and that they would face Justice. That made her happy. Between the ones who had used her as an example, and the ones who had not intervened, she had no warm feelings for any of them.

She was free now. She could do anything she wanted, and her mind was full of paintings in a riot of colors. She wanted to make beautiful art. She'd figure out the rest later.

She found the shop quickly and took her time as she pored over the materials available. There were notebooks with thick paper, good for watery paints, and boards that would take thicker paints nicely. Some brushes were so soft, she could hardly believe they were real.

And the *paints*…

They were here in every color she could imagine and more, and when she opened the lids surreptitiously, the smell brought her back to some of the happiest times in her life. When she painted, she found she could accept the universe as it was. Her own story faded into a larger universe that still held beauty. The smell brought all of that back.

Even though she'd been rich, she had tried to use as little of her family's wealth as possible. She'd never bought good paints or brushes, in part because she didn't want to feel gratitude to Mustafee for anything, but also because she superstitiously feared that if she cared too much for her paintings, Mustafee would have used that against her, too.

She didn't have to fear that now. Recklessly, she bought everything she wanted from the shop and loaded herself up with bags that Jeltor offered to carry—and then complained about as they made their way back down the stairs to the clothing boutiques.

There weren't many clothes here that fit Yofu, but she cared less about that. Tafa selected things in plain blacks and greys, reminiscent of the clothes Barnabas wore around the ship—it was an elegant look without too much effort, which appealed to her—and then bought some toiletries.

"What do you need?" she asked Jeltor.

"Oh, are you done?" His tone was acid. "Or would you like to load me up with some more bags?"

"*You're* not even carrying them," Tafa pointed out. "The suit is."

"And it's straining at the joints. I need oil and fittings. They're one level down from the main floor."

"Well, let's go, then." Tafa rolled her eyes as the Jotun stomped past her. Jeltor really just liked to complain. He'd been nicer to her over the past few days, and she guessed that part of it was that Barnabas had promised to return him to the Jotun fleet, where Jeltor's family still lived. He'd been on a work trip when he was captured.

Her smiled faded when she thought of the people on their ship who hadn't survived the attack. She and Jeltor had been lucky. If Drakuz'd had the chance to sell them, their lives would be very different right now.

They'd just passed the main floor when there was a shout. Several figures raced across the main room, and a few moments later, they heard shots fired.

The people screamed and cowered, but she only crossed her arms and watched as the figures ran to the far end of the level and disappeared.

"Oh, good," Jeltor said sarcastically. "We'll be imprisoned as part of Barnabas' crew."

"He's not in jail yet," Tafa pointed out. "It seems like he does this everywhere he goes. So we're probably fine. We should get back to the ship, though."

"Leaving *my* supplies unpurchased. Of course."

"Yeah, yeah. They gave you a tune-up, and you've been running better than ever. No complaining."

Crallus had tried his very best to forget Barnabas, the Yennai Corporation, and even Uleq.

The food helped. It was some of the best he'd ever eaten. The meat was tender. The drinks were paired perfectly. The vegetables were fresh. Who got to eat like this on a station, much less for free? He devoted all his attention to it and pretended this was a celebration of a successful job.

You know, rather than remember that his whole team died, and he was sitting with a cold-blooded murderer who might get Crallus killed.

He'd just finished when Uleq's head jerked up, and Crallus felt his stomach drop. He looked around with a sense of deep misgiving.

Barnabas was staring at them with a small smile on his face.

Crallus didn't hesitate.

"*Run.*" He grabbed Uleq's arm and yanked him out of his seat.

The Torcellan hissed in anger at being hurt this way,

but it was more for form's sake than anything else. He'd frozen in surprise, but like Crallus, he knew that if they got caught they were going to die.

"Stop him!" Crallus yelled at the guards. He pointed at Barnabas. "He's trying to assassinate one of the Yennai Corporation's heirs!"

"I'm not an heir!" Uleq yelled as they sprinted across the main floor. Gunshots rang out behind them.

"They don't need to know that!" Crallus called back.

Rich people. It was like they were born without common sense.

His shoulder ached, but he pushed the thought away. He had to keep running. They had to get to the ship before Barnabas caught them.

He'd seen some of the security footage from the syndicate base, and it had made his blood run cold. This human was a creature of nightmares and Crallus was terrified to die as painfully as his soldiers had.

He felt guilty for leaving them. But not guilty enough to accept retribution from a monster with glowing red eyes.

Guards swarmed out of nowhere, and Barnabas' eyes narrowed.

"My quarrel is not with you. Step aside."

They thought they had seen everything, the idiots. All of them reached for their weapons in an obvious display of force.

"Sir," the guard captain started. "We're going to have to ask you to leave."

Barnabas took a moment to sigh. Then he launched himself into their midst, dispatching them with brutal efficiency. "Gar, keep an eye on Crallus and Uleq."

Gar started to run after them, only to get lifted over a guard's head and brought down hard on the floor. He yelped, and Barnabas tried to refrain from sighing again.

Tunnel vision was common in a fight—focusing on one enemy to the exclusion of others. Gar knew he was lucky that his lesson had been in the form of pain because quite often, the consequences of tunnel vision were fatal.

Barnabas knocked out as many of the guards as he could, but they weren't making it easy. They charged him with impressive technique and tactics. They'd clearly been trained to take on elite assassins, which Barnabas supposed made sense given the nature of their business. None of their training had been for combatants enhanced with Kurtherian DNA and technology, however, and they fell one and two at a time until Barnabas faced down the last of them: the guard captain.

"Stand aside," he said again.

The guard captain's eyes narrowed, and a feral yell burst from his lips. He charged at Barnabas in a fury, snarling either insults or threats in his native language. Probably some combination of both. Barnabas didn't understand the words, but the general meaning behind them was clear.

Barnabas' intentions were just as clear. He'd readied his knives when the guard captain was tackled sideways. Gar slammed into him and carried him down, following up with a flurry of punches at the Shrillexian's head.

In fairness to the Shrillexian, Barnabas would have to

say that shock probably did part of Gar's job for him. The guard captain must have thought he was hallucinating when he saw that it was a Luvendi who had tackled him and was presently beating the living shit out of him.

That said, Gar acquitted himself nicely. In a footnote to what would become a legendary day on Virtue Station, he proceeded to completely incapacitate the guard captain. He stood up, chest heaving, and then—as the battered, bruised captain reached for his gun—shot the Shrillexian.

"Good job." Barnabas was already on the move. "Come on," he called over his shoulder.

Gar raced after him. Crallus and Uleq had just reached the far side of the main floor, heading toward the ramps that led to the docking bays, when Barnabas put on a burst of speed that left Gar in the dust.

"Shinigami, stop any ships from leaving!"

"I'm trying." Shinigami's voice betrayed her worry. "They've got another system I didn't know about, though. Probably just for Yennai higher-ups. It's on a completely different encryption system and—"

"Less talking, more hacking!" Barnabas burst through the doors with his guns already out and skidded into cover as a hail of gunfire shot overhead. He could hear screams behind him as some of the bullets went through the open doors, and he felt a wave of fury. The people on the banking floor might generally be scum, but they didn't deserve a random death from a stray bullet. That wasn't Justice. "Shinigami, the ship is pulling away. Follow it!"

"I'm trying! They've got manual clamps locked down on every other ship in the station. If I try to pull away, I'll tear the hull—or vent the docking bay."

"Goddammit!" Barnabas grabbed Gar as the Luvendi came through the doors and pulled him down. Only three guards were shooting, and he picked them off methodically before standing.

"We lost them." Gar looked incredulous. "We fought, but they got away."

Barnabas reached out to clasp his shoulder and was about to say a few words about best efforts and frustration when one of the dock workers laughed.

"You're a Luvendi," the dockworker told Gar. "If *you* were fighting, that's the reason they got away."

Gar's face went cold, and he turned slowly. "Take. That. Back."

Uh-oh, Barnabas murmured privately to Shinigami.

Uh-oh? No, this gon' be gooood. Her frustration forgotten, Shinigami brought up all the feeds she could find of the docking bay. *Get some popcorn. There's gonna be a fight.*

13

"Gar." Barnabas' voice was deep and even. "This isn't worth fighting about."

It's totally worth fighting about.

Shinigami!

What? He got insulted.

Gar could hardly hear them through the pounding of his blood in his ears. He narrowed his eyes at the dock-worker, a stupid-looking Hieto with piggy eyes and a crooked snout. He was still laughing at Gar, and he nodded in Barnabas' direction.

"You should listen to your friend, Luvendi." He turned away, clearly having decided that neither of them was going to shoot him, but that Barnabas also wasn't going to make a big deal of the insult.

He should have just kept walking. Everyone agreed on that point later. Gar might have been talked down if he'd shut up and gone away.

On the other hand, it made such a good story that everyone decided it was better the Hieto hadn't resisted getting one last shot in. "Where'd you find someone to make you armor, anyway? They were laughing at you the whole time, you skinny bastard. You paid them for nothing."

"Shut. Up." The words came out as a snarl.

"Oooh, good one." The Hieto looked back and forth between Barnabas and Gar. "You see this, human? Is he actually on your team? What'd he say to get you to—"

Gar's punch caught him on the side of the head, and the Hieto dropped in a heap. All across the docking bay, workers who'd pretended not to watch stopped pretending. A sea of faces turned in their direction.

"I think you showed him," Barnabas said gently.

"No, you didn't. Make an example, Gar."

Shinigami, if you don't shut up—

What, you'll turn this ship around? I fly the ship.

As the dockworkers edged closer, Gar sank into a crouch and watched the Hieto's unconscious form. When at last he came to, shaking his head muzzily and pushing himself up on his hands and knees, Gar stood and kicked him in his plated stomach.

Ohhhhhhh. Did you get popcorn yet? Because I reiterate: this gon' be good.

I can't decide if I'm worried or...

Or you really, really want to see this? Shinigami asked slyly.

Barnabas sighed. *Yes.*

I knew it. Sit back and enjoy, Big B.

From the look of surprise as he tipped over, no one had ever kicked the Hieto hard enough to knock the wind out of him. Given his armored scales, he could certainly be forgiven for not being used to the experience.

The larger surprise, however, was almost certain that a Luvendi had done it.

"Get up," Gar spat. "You want to say I can't fight? Fight me, then. I think you can see from those two hits that I have what it takes."

"Exactly," Barnabas started. "So we should really—"

So help me, God, if you get him to leave instead of fighting I will never forgive you.

The last thing we need is to start some sort of legend.

Tooooo late.

It was indeed too late. The Hieto stood up, gave a nervous laugh, and must have decided that his memory of Gar's punch simply hadn't happened. He looked around, assumed that the hits must have come from Barnabas, and tried to charge him.

Gar tackled him before he got two steps. He stood, hauled the Hieto off the floor, and slammed him back down again. From the sound of it, more than one scale cracked.

Everyone flinched, even Barnabas.

"I was the one who punched you. I was the one who kicked you." Gar narrowed his eyes. "I was the one who killed the guard captain back there."

Oh, no, Barnabas said.

Yeah, I think it's safe to say we're not going to be welcome here anymore. Of course, it's not like they don't have facial recognition cameras.

Well, I suppose that's true.

But I am warming up the engines now that the manual locks are off.

Good call. Barnabas cleared his throat. "Gar, we should go."

"In a moment." Gar's eyes were narrowed. "He tried to shame me."

"And *you* know that he's not correct about you," Barnabas retorted.

For the record, I don't think that's going to work.

Why not?

How many centuries did it take before you stopped responding when people questioned your *manliness?*

Do you think that often happens in monasteries?

You weren't always in monasteries!

Yes, I see your point. Barnabas sighed. *I wish we weren't drawing attention to him yet. A Luvendi who can fight? That's noteworthy.*

Between you being you and the name of this ship, I think the boat has already sailed on us being low-key.

The Hieto struggled up and gave Gar an unfriendly look. "So you can fight," he sneered. "Maybe. But you can't expect people to—" His voice broke off in a squawk as Gar clamped a hand around his throat.

Gar dragged him close. "Manners!"

Oh, Lord, he's beginning to talk like you.

I sound like a prat.

Since you bring it up—

We'll discuss this later.

The Hieto struggled and choked.

"The people you let get away are mass-murderers," Gar said angrily. "You mock me when you did not stop them, either. They would gladly sell you into slavery. They abandoned hundreds of their own to get massacred just last week. And instead of taking the time to learn any of this, you decided to mock those who were attempting to bring them to Justice."

"Who the hell are you?" the Hieto spat.

"I am Venfaldri Gar."

"How did you—"

"None. Of. Your. Business." Gar released his fingers and let the Hieto drop to the floor. "Apologize."

"No."

Had he not said that one word, things might have gone differently. Gar could have made a suitably dramatic exit, and the Hieto wouldn't have spent the next few weeks in a body cast.

But again, everyone agreed that the story was much better this way.

Gar paused, tilting his head to the side much the way Barnabas did. "I beg your pardon?"

"I said no. You come from a weak race." The Hieto hauled itself up. "Your people are weak and useless. They're grifters. They make nothing of their own."

Gar let loose. His knuckles slammed into the Hieto's face over and over, blocking the Hieto's strikes easily.

I should probably—oh—do something about—OH—breaking this up. That one had to hurt. Lesson learned: Hieto scales sound awful when they crack.

Ewwww, Shinigami agreed.

The Hieto was sprawled on the floor, hissing in defiance but clearly defeated, and at last, the anger drained from Gar.

"You'll get yourself killed if you keep doing that," he told the Hieto. He turned and left, shaking his head as Barnabas followed.

He threw a few coins to one of the other dock workers. "Get your friend some medical help and talk some sense into him."

The dock worker said nothing, and Barnabas hurried Gar along to the *Shinigami*.

"Why are we running?"

"Because someone's going to call the guards," Barnabas said. "That's what tends to happen when there's a fight. Especially after a fight where several station-hired guards get killed."

"Oh."

"Yes. Oh." Barnabas was glad to see Tafa and Jeltor already on board as they arrived. "Any problems?" he asked them.

"Tafa bought half the station and made me carry it," Jeltor said in tones of deep martyrdom.

"That is *not* true." Tafa gave him an annoyed look before looking at Barnabas. "I got some paints! And boards and notebooks and brushes and—oh. We saw people running and heard gunshots."

"Yes, that was us," Barnabas admitted, his amusement evident. "Everything is fine. Although we should probably leave before someone calls the authorities."

"Already undocking," Shinigami reported.

"Good." Barnabas nodded. "Let's get out of here."

Zinqued was forcing his way through another cup of Stim-Drink when the message flashed up on his screen.

SHINIGAMI SPOTTED AT VIRTUE STATION. JUST UNDOCKED. HEADING FOR QUADRANT 982.

Zinqued gave a cold smile and sat up straight, his exhaustion forgotten. He punched in the coordinates, and his smile grew as the ship began to turn. Paun probably wouldn't notice for a few hours, and by then they'd be well on the way.

Easier to ask forgiveness than permission.

14

"There's a warrant out for our arrest at Virtue Station," Shinigami reported. "Of course, not *exactly* for us." Her avatar was leaning against the wall as Gar and Barnabas warmed up on the mats. "Also, is painting in a gym a normal Yofu activity?"

"Hmm?" Barnabas, who was stretching, looked up curiously.

Tafa, who was painting in the corner, looked up at the cameras with her left eye. "They inspire me."

Shinigami snorted to show what she thought of that. Jeltor agreed with a mechanical-sounding sigh.

"*Anyway*," Shinigami continued. "It turns out that the guard captain for Jodu's bank was a real piece of work. He would just go around murdering people. They knew that it was a human and a Luvendi, and they have the security tapes, but once people heard that *Gar* was the one who'd killed the guard captain, they started going to the guards and claiming they knew stuff. You know, adding in details.

So the report out says that Gar was wearing a disguise but was actually a Leath. You're a Torcellan, apparently. We have a crew of Shrillexians, our ship name is really the *Calcifer*, and we're legendary for starting a blood feud that ended with us wiping out an entire family of bankers."

"It's like Robin Hood," Barnabas said drily. "Except with less distribution of wealth and more wild lies."

"You think Robin Hood just *stole*? He totally killed people. But I think you two have really hit on something here: you kill bankers, and all the normal people are just going to claim they didn't see anything."

"That won't really work," Gar interjected. He was limbering up as he stared at Barnabas and tried to come up with some strategy that wouldn't result in a great deal of pain.

"You should look up Charles Floyd in the history banks," Shinigami suggested.

"We are not becoming petty criminals," Barnabas declared.

"Of course not. We don't steal $20 bills. We murder people."

"We *judge* people."

"Legally speaking—"

"Yes, yes," Barnabas said hastily. Under his breath, however, he added, "With you egging Gar on."

"There were reasons for what I did," Shinigami said in lofty tones.

"See?" Gar told Barnabas. "There were reasons."

Barnabas gave him a pitying look. "Ask her what they are."

"Uh, Shinigami—"

"It was *hilarious.*" Shinigami was completely unrepentant.

"You said it was because he insulted me!"

"And it would be hilarious if you beat him up. I was right, too. It *was* hilarious. You're a hero now. All of a sudden, a Luvendi is going around beating up awful people and helping out the little guys. And trust me, your species could use some good PR. I'm helping."

"Your help is entirely incidental," Barnabas said. "Come on, Gar. Time to spar."

Gar groaned—this was going to hurt. Every time they sparred, Barnabas gave him more pointers, which Gar dutifully put into action.

The thing was, he still never came even *close* to winning. Sidestepping one hit didn't keep him from being hopelessly outmatched in speed, strength, and tactics. Barnabas just repeated that Gar was learning important things.

Gar kept pointing out that learning didn't really help him if he never had a chance of winning.

But, for reasons he could not figure out, he kept coming back, and it was entirely on him—Barnabas never asked about sparring. He simply went to the gym each day as he always had and trained on his own. If Gar showed up, Barnabas was courteous. It was only if Gar stepped onto the mats and asked to spar that Barnabas would do so.

So Gar had only himself to blame for the bruises he was about to receive.

He gave a little sigh as he bounced on the balls of his

feet and considered if he should circle or just rush Barnabas—

He wasn't entirely sure what happened, but he opened his eyes to find himself looking up at the ceiling. "Ow."

"Get up." Barnabas was clearly trying to control his amusement. "And spend less time thinking when you're in the ring."

"Mmf." Gar pushed himself up. This time, Barnabas' attack dragged Gar across the mats and slammed him into the wall. Barnabas had his hand at Gar's throat, and his blue eyes had a twinkle of amusement, which somehow managed to be almost as intimidating as his red-eyed, blood-covered battle incarnation.

"This is *great*." Tafa's brush was dancing over the twin canvases. "Keep it up, you two. I haven't been this inspired in ages."

Even Barnabas looked a little unsettled by that.

"I say we just put a kill switch in her," Shinigami suggested.

Gar gave a wide-eyed nod at her avatar.

"Chief?"

"I'm not going to agree to that."

"I notice you do not disagree, either."

"Well, no."

Shinigami chuckled in their heads as Barnabas released Gar and the two started to circle again. "Also," she said over the speakers, "we should talk about those programs at Virtue Station."

"Which— Oh, the ones that kept you out?" Barnabas shot a quick frown at Shinigami's avatar.

"Mmm. I may not have been *entirely* honest at the time."

Barnabas said nothing. He simply waited as Gar launched a flurry of kicks at him. He blocked each one, pointedly not looking at Shinigami until she cleared her throat hastily—an amusing mannerism that seemed as natural to her now as Tabitha—and explained.

"Their systems aren't sentient, but they're *very* aggressive, and they're partitioned into multiple distinct servers."

"What, physical servers?" Barnabas launched himself up, pushed off the wall, and flipped over Gar's head. As Gar whirled around, confused, Barnabas grabbed him and spun him around the axis of his shoulders before setting him back on his feet and knocking the wind out of him. Gar wobbled, turned around in a circle, and fell with a squeak.

"This is *great*," Tafa murmured again. She poured out some new paints onto her palette. "Green. Definitely green."

"You hear that?" Shinigami asked, flickering across the room to lean over Gar. "Your pain is green."

"Blrgle."

"*Up*," Barnabas commanded. He took Gar's hand and hauled the Luvendi to his feet. "Again. This time try not to let me throw you."

"That sounds doable."

Barnabas fixed him with a look. "It *is* doable. You're convinced you can't beat me, but that's not true."

"It's true," Shinigami, Tafa, and Jeltor said in unison.

"The three of you aren't helping, you know."

Gar, however, seemed galvanized by their disbelief. He shook his head to clear it and nodded. "No, they're right. I can't...yet. Let's go again."

"Mmm." Barnabas sank into a crouch and began to circle.

Again, Gar charged, and again, Barnabas launched himself toward the same wall to push up. However, this time Gar changed direction sharply and punched his leg out to catch Barnabas just as he landed. Barnabas staggered sideways and grabbed for Gar's leg, but Gar was out of range, circling again.

"Good," Barnabas called. "That was good. Now, this time—"

Gar didn't wait for the rest of it. He charged, dodged Barnabas' first attempted throw—

And wound up upside down against the far wall, barely catching himself with his hands before he crashed to the floor.

There was the distant sound of an alert and Shinigami's avatar fuzzed briefly out of existence. When she came back, she was frowning. "We have company."

"I'll be on the bridge." Barnabas grabbed his towel and made for the door. "Tafa, Jeltor, you secure yourselves in your rooms. No, Tafa, *leave* the painting."

"But it's some of my best work—"

"Nope." Barnabas ushered her out the sliding doors. "Gar?"

"I should have stayed on Luvendan," Gar said, staring at the ceiling with a look of poetic sadness. "And been eaten by the Essekan."

"Mmm." Barnabas ushered Tafa and Jeltor out, hiding his smile, and left Gar in peace.

Shinigami's avatar flickered over to lie on the floor with Gar. She even had her legs up the wall, the same as his. She pillowed her hands behind her head and pursed her lips. Whistling came from the speakers.

"I can't tell you how comforting your friendship is in this painful time," Gar said. He was trying to be sarcastic, but his lips were twitching in a genuine smile.

"Ahhhh, you're laughing. Go on, you know you want to. Come on, get up." She pushed herself up and offered him a hand, then snatched it away. "Sorry, I always see people do that. Forgot my hand's not actually there."

Gar pushed himself up with a laugh. "Right. I didn't fracture anything, did I?"

"Nope. You're good to go as soon as we deal with these asshats."

"Oof. Take your time, then."

On the bridge, Barnabas slid into the captain's chair. "Are Tafa and Jeltor in their rooms?"

"Yes." Shinigami appeared and sat as well. She looked at him to see what he thought of the human mannerism and smiled when he nodded. It had become one of their games for him to assess how human her movements looked. She settled back in the chair. "Tafa is still complaining about that painting. If we can get out of this without doing any barrel rolls, we really should. I don't want to listen to her moan on about losing it."

Barnabas smiled slightly. He sensed that the truth was that Shinigami did not want to hurt Tafa's feelings by ruining the painting. And when Shinigami willingly chose not to use fancy battle techniques to protect someone's feelings, that was a high compliment to them indeed.

"So, what's going on?" Barnabas asked. He knew if he

mentioned Shinigami's kindness, she would only get embarrassed and prickly. "What was the alert for?"

"There's a ship following us." She pulled up the video feed.

Barnabas squinted. Strangely, even in plain vision, the ship was barely visible.

"They're good at this," Shinigami observed. Her face was watchful, eyes slightly narrowed as she considered. "They must suspect that we did a visual check on the debris last time, so they're following somewhere they won't be easy to see, either by the naked eye or on our sensors. If I wasn't built as well as I was..."

Barnabas looked at her for a moment. Rarely did Shinigami refer to the ship as her body, but it must feel that way to her. He wondered what that must be like.

"So what's their plan?"

"That's the question, isn't it?" She arched a single eyebrow, so like Bethany Anne in her mannerisms for a moment that it was jarring.

Then he noticed the avatar looked a little different. He wasn't sure—but her features were a touch less aquiline, her skin closer to a healthy human shade, and the hair was silver now, not pure white.

Interesting.

There was a pause while Barnabas squinted at the ship. "I don't suppose we've seen this one before."

"Not that I know of, and it isn't balanced the way a warship would be. That's the good news. The bad news is that there are a lot of ships like this and they tend to have a rather nasty suite of tricks to steal other ships."

"Steal?" Barnabas looked over at her sharply. "There was that net a while ago."

"Mmm. It's definitely a nice coincidence, but these outer quadrants are *filled* with people who steal ships for a living."

"I told Tik'ta to spread the word that our ship was not to be preyed on," Barnabas groused.

"And while she may have done exactly as you asked, it's possible that *other* people took that as more of a challenge than a warning."

Barnabas groaned. "I always forget how stupid people are."

"This ship is incredibly valuable. There will always be people who go for the most difficult thing. I understand a lot of people used to climb Mount Everest despite the risks."

"A good point, although—"

There was a flicker on the screen.

"They've launched something," Shinigami said.

The two of them leaned toward one of the screens and watched as the object grew closer. It was so small that even their sensors hardly picked it up.

"A bomb?" Barnabas asked.

"I don't think so. And frankly..." She looked at him with a sharp-toothed smile. "I'm curious. I say we let it do whatever it wants to do."

"Risky, Shinigami."

"You want to know just as much as I do." Her smile said *checkmate.*

Barnabas grumbled, but the truth was that he *did* want to know. "Close the blast doors, then, and make sure it hits somewhere there aren't passengers. We'd better hope this isn't EMP."

"I can deal with EMP." Shinigami looked over as the bridge doors slid open and Gar limped in. "Good of you to join us. We're about to be hit."

"*By what?*" Gar hurried to strap himself in.

"There's a ship," Barnabas said, gesturing to the screens. "Shinigami, what's the ETA on— Never mind." A loud *thunk* echoed through the ship.

A moment later, Shinigami announced, outraged, "It's drilling through my *hull!*"

"Yes, well, you wanted to see what would happen. Is it trying to vent the ship?"

"No, it's stopping near the first circuit of electrical —ohhhhh."

Barnabas raised an eyebrow.

"They're trying to hack us," Shinigami said. "The device clamps on, drills in, and tries to get into the system. Oh, that tickles."

"Tickles?"

"It's like my mind itches." She wrinkled her nose. "Oh, they're so cute. They think they can hack me. Have they never heard of Etheric Empire AIs?"

"Most people haven't. It's not something we try to spread around."

"So you're telling me I can't give them a big speech about how they fucked up."

"Pretty much. Just deal with them."

Shinigami sighed. "Fine." She frowned for a moment and closed her eyes in a spot-on impression of a human meditating. A few moments later, her eyes snapped open and she spoke.

Even knowing that she was not speaking to them, Barnabas and Gar shivered.

"Your pathetic little device is not even close to hurting this ship," Shinigami said. "It is so pathetic, in fact, that I cannot even bring myself to shoot your ship down. It would be dishonorable to do so. Go eat some paste and reconsider your career path."

Gar leaned over to Barnabas and murmured, "Eat some paste?"

Barnabas stifled his laugh. "It's an Earth saying. Too much to explain. It means they're stupid."

"Ah." Gar looked faintly sad. "So she's really not going to blow their ship up?"

"Maybe I should stop you two from hanging out so much without direct supervision," Barnabas said with a sigh. "You two bring out the worst in each other."

"Or the best," Shinigami and Gar responded in unison as the *Shinigami* put on a burst of speed and left their pursuer in the dust.

Zinqued and Chofal stared at one another in consternation. They were both still wide-eyed from the message they had received.

"What do you think it means to eat paste?" Chofal asked finally.

"I don't know," Zinqued admitted. "But they're weak if

they're not going to shoot us down. It means we have another chance."

"*Zinqued—*"

"I'm *getting* that ship." Zinqued jabbed a finger at her. "I'm *getting* it."

Chofal groaned. Next time, Paun might find out about what they had done, and they'd both get fired.

That was assuming the ship didn't just shoot them down next time.

15

"So, the question is..." Barnabas brought up a holographic map of the quadrants that were relatively nearby. "Where is Uleq going?"

"We're just asking that now?" Gar wondered.

Jeltor made a mechanical-sounding grumble of agreement.

"His ship was launched from a different set of systems than the main ones used on Virtue Station," Barnabas explained. "They're entirely partitioned, which means that Shinigami wasn't able to get a toehold into them. All we have is their initial trajectory. She's been working on finding more, but..."

"But they're tricky sonsabitches," Shinigami said succinctly. Her avatar frowned as it looked at the map. "They can't hide everything from me, but they knew enough to hide a good deal of it. They've run some of the YCS ship departures through the main system, or possibly fed it false data with some *heavy* encryption, so if you're looking at it, it doesn't *look* like they'd have a second set of systems."

Her avatar flickered and disappeared after that. Shinigami wasn't in the mood to play human. She didn't particularly want anyone looking at her.

She was *pissed.* She had thought she was making headway against the Yennai Corporation, and instead, they'd played her. It wasn't personal, of course, but she still didn't like coming in second to her opponents.

Not to mention letting down her friends.

"I guess they knew they'd make a very, very powerful enemy someday," Barnabas said. He'd surmised the flow of Shinigami's thoughts and was careful to steer the conversation free either of blame or absolution.

All that mattered was taking their enemies down. They would suffer setbacks and defeats, Barnabas knew. He was not foolish enough to think that they would always come out ahead. Indeed, he had learned over the years that failure was absolutely necessary for the long run.

Only with the taste of defeat would people strive to push the limits of what they could do, and only by pushing those limits could they hope to triumph when the stakes were high.

In this case, he knew that the Yennai Corporation was a cannier opponent than they had guessed. The organic structure surrounded a fierce and ruthless organization. He brought up the list of color-coded planets and stations. Red—where the corporation had enemies, Blue—where they had known agents, and Green, where they had a controlling stake. The glowing dots highlighted nearly every major system, including many capital planets for various alien species.

"This is the Yennai Corporation," Barnabas explained. "Anything that gets this big is subject to many forces. As an organization, it will begin to command loyalty beyond simply what its leaders ask for. It is essentially a living thing now. It has made itself integral to the economic, security, and political systems of this entire sector. People will instinctively defend it."

Shinigami's avatar appeared again, this time no more than ten inches tall. She walked slowly through the holographic map, reaching out sometimes to touch various glimmers. Today, all hints of Tabitha's features were gone, and she was pure Bethany Anne, from the determined mouth to the watchful eyes.

Barnabas watched her for a moment. She was clearly pondering the situation, and he guessed that she would tell them her conclusions only when they were close to finished. The way she interacted with the map looked almost random at this point, and he presumed that her instincts were guiding her toward a solution.

He cleared his throat to draw the team's focus back to him. Whatever Shinigami was processing, she clearly didn't want to be the center of attention right now.

"Often, organizations like this will get very big without any real plan. They simply want profits and political influence. They'll lobby governments and give bribes. Those organizations have vulnerabilities that come from not really considering security at the start.

"Yennai is different. It's beginning to look like they

always planned to run this sector of space. They've been treating themselves as a government, making deliberate attempts to obtain the things governments need—a banking system, an army, mainframes with very high levels of security, and misdirection. I'm wondering if they intended to take over various governments one by one and fight the ones they couldn't assimilate."

"I wouldn't be surprised," Jeltor cut in. "They've been angling to get agents into the Jotun government for a year. They're bold."

Barnabas raised his eyebrows.

"I was there when Get'ruz Shipping joined the Yennai Corporation," Jeltor said drily. "The Yennai delegates… well, they talked us down. One of the Get'ruz captains had struck at our supply chain, and we were about to make an example of them when a few Yennai ships showed up pretty much out of nowhere and started negotiating." His jellyfish body swiveled slightly as he looked around at all of them from the clear tank at the power suit's center. "It didn't look like they had many weapons on those ships or even good shielding capabilities, but it would have been suicidal to go into that situation without either, and I never got the impression that they were stupid."

Shinigami paused in her map-wandering to look at him. She had found versions of this story alluded to in the syndicate files, but she hadn't heard it told like this.

"They showed up and told the syndicate that if they joined the corporation, they'd be protected," she reported. "I got the sense it was something they did a lot."

"I wouldn't be surprised," Jeltor said. "They acted like it

was the most natural thing for a business representative to put themselves between two armed fleets and start negotiating for peace." He snorted. "*Peace.* It was just profit. They showed up a few weeks later on Jevvendi to start asking about trade deals."

Barnabas watched him. Jeltor betrayed the inborn prejudices that had helped Yennai fly under the radar. Jeltor and the rest of the Jotun Navy had correctly guessed that the Yennai Corporation had a dangerous fleet.

And yet, when looking back at the incident, they assumed that Yennai wanted nothing more than money.

Barnabas thought back to Uleq's run-in with Bethany Anne. As he studied the map in front of him, he became even more convinced that money was only part of what the Yennai Corporation wanted.

They wanted power—and the more he knew of them, the more he was sure that they absolutely should not have it. Whatever their endgame was, it was dangerous.

"There's a message coming in," Shinigami reported. "Jeltor, it's a reply to the one you sent earlier."

Jeltor's body swung sharply to look at the avatar. "You intercepted that? How?" He sounded agitated.

"You used my systems to send it," Shinigami pointed out.

"The encryption should have been unbreakable." And his tone had more than a hint of complaint to it. Clearly, Jeltor did not like the idea that they were spying on him.

Shinigami disappeared and appeared once more as a normally-sized human. She gave Jeltor an amused look. "From the high grade of weaponry on your suit, and the built-in encryption and messaging systems, I guessed you were part of the Jotun military—or at least upper class."

Jeltor remained silent.

"It would be irresponsible for me *not* to monitor your communications," she pointed out. "Especially when they were going to Jotun high command. And, since you had tried to hack me."

Barnabas looked at Jeltor with raised eyebrows.

To his surprise, the Jotun acceded with good grace. "Can you agree, at least, that it would be irresponsible for me *not* to attempt to assess your capabilities?" he asked Shinigami. His body swiveled as he looked at Barnabas. "You've been instrumental in taking out any number of ships recently, and yet the Etheric Empire is no more. Trying to find out your allegiances and your capabilities was important."

"You could have asked," Barnabas pointed out mildly. "We've been nothing if not kind to you."

But he could tell from the Jotun's thoughts that he'd told the truth. As the days had worn on, Jeltor had become less guarded. He seemed to be more at ease in Barnabas' presence, and often forgot to shield his thoughts. Barnabas had also learned to interpret the Jotun's thoughts through the strange feel of them.

Jeltor had, indeed, been worried about what Barnabas intended to do in this sector.

"With all due respect," Jeltor began. "A soldier doesn't rely on words and explanations, but actions. Yours... have set me at ease, but I could not say I completely understand them. It is disconcerting, in someone with such weaponry." Then he remembered Shinigami's previous statement. "Shinigami, you said there was a message?"

"Yes. It's just text, it simply says you are correct in your guess." To Barnabas, Shinigami added, *His message was easy enough to decrypt, but even then, it was oblique.*

"You could hardly expect the Jotun Navy to send messages that were easily deciphered," Jeltor scoffed. He sounded pleased by the message, however. "I had a hunch when we were at Virtue Station. You see, we saw Uleq and Crallus fleeing across the main floor from one of the banks. They knew they were being chased. There would be no reason for them to do anything other than switch ships…unless someone in the Yennai Corporation who outranked them had demanded it."

Barnabas made a faint sound of satisfaction.

"I suggested as much to my colleagues, who looked into it." Jeltor laid a small data disk on the table in front of Barnabas, and after Shinigami scanned it and gave the okay, Barnabas plugged it into the table.

The map disappeared, and several Torcellan faces appeared with dossiers. Jeltor pointed to the one in the very center of the display.

"This is Ilia Yennai. She is the heir to the Yennai Corporation and has proven herself a good leader, but her father still holds the bulk of the control in the company. It was my hunch that *she* was the one who ordered Uleq detained, and it would seem I was correct."

"Why?" Barnabas asked.

"*That,* I don't know." Jeltor sounded pensive now. "Ilia's a nasty character, and she's been the heir for years. If you wanted someone ruthless as your successor, she'd be a good choice. The thing is, Uleq isn't anyone to disregard, either. He's been bouncing around for years, involving himself in various schemes, and while he hasn't *yet* done anything like take down someone of your Empress's caliber, he's gotten closer than blind luck would allow." He looked directly at Barnabas. "If you want my guess, I'd say that he's closer to becoming heir than Ilia wants, and she's determined to take him down."

"Interesting." Barnabas looked at Ilia's face. She shared some of the same features as her brother, whose dossier hovered in the air. Their father was shown with what must be a very old photo. "What do we know about the father?"

"Almost nothing," Jeltor answered. "He started the corporation when he was quite young and basically disappeared from the public eye. Honestly, it's possible he's no longer alive, and Ilia's just pretending he is for some reason. I'd say that's unlikely, but he hasn't been seen in years."

"Hmmm."

"In any event," Jeltor went on smoothly, "while we can't tell you where their main base would be—we've been trying for years to figure it out—we can tell you what kind of weaponry you'll find there if you ever track them down. Part of the message we received was giving me clearance to reveal that information."

Barnabas smiled. "What a coincidence," he said. "We just happen to know where their base is. I'm guessing if we were to go take it out...Jotun high command wouldn't exactly be upset."

"Not at all." Jeltor sounded pleased. "They're worried at how many of our politicians seem to have been bribed.

Take them out, and you won't have any interference from our Navy."

"I think that's settled then." Barnabas looked at Shinigami. "Set a course, and let's figure out how to take out this base."

16

Zinqued lounged in the ship's tiny rec room with a few other members of the crew, playing a new game called 'checkers,' when Paun strode into the room in a fury.

"Did you think you would just get away with it?" he demanded.

Zinqued shot a hard look at Chofal, who gave a tiny, terrified shake of her head. She hadn't told Paun what happened.

Paun saw the look, and his lips tightened in anger. "I reviewed the ship's logs," he said contemptuously. "I saw that we pursued a ship last night and that you launched something. I saw the record of the message that came in from the human. Why would you take such a risk? You know how dangerous that human ship is."

"If we catch that ship—" Zinqued began.

Paun barked. "Don't tell me again that we'll be rich if we catch the ship. I spent a long time assembling a crew that wasn't stupid enough to do things like that—or, I thought I did. The people who go for the big prizes are the ones who get killed. They get greedy, and greedy people get stupid, and stupid people get dead. Are you stupid, Zinqued?"

Zinqued stood up. Anger pounded in his blood.

"How long since we've caught a ship?" He stared Paun down. "We haven't had a haul in weeks. You said yourself that good catches are getting fewer and farther between. Catch this one, and we're set for months—years, even."

Paun's face was still unfriendly, but he didn't look as sure anymore. "Just because we haven't had a good take doesn't mean we should do something stupid," he said.

But the weakness was there.

Zinqued pressed his advantage. "We don't have to do something stupid. We know what kinds of tricks they can see through now, and we have information about the other people they took down. We can learn their weaknesses and set a trap for them."

Paun crossed his arms. He was listening, and so was the rest of the crew.

"They have good detection systems," Zinqued explained. "So we need to arrange an ambush somewhere they won't be able to see us coming. There are places nearby with electromagnetic interference or a lot of radio traffic. We'd want to find one of those. Their anti-hacking systems are top-notch, so we can't rely on hacking to bring the ship under control. We need to use good, old-fashioned manual controls."

He snuck a glance at Paun and was pleased to see the other alien looked amenable to this.

"Finally," Zinqued resumed. "We know they can fire multiple spreads of weapons at once, but that they don't like to hurt innocent ships. My suggestion would be to get multiple mercenary ships and disguise them as cargo or transport ships, meaning that the *Shinigami* won't fire on them. A few of them will be able to dock, and board and they can overpower the relatively small crew."

He'd almost had it, but now Paun's brows snapped together.

"Multiple mercenary ships?" Paun sounded halfway between incredulous and absolutely filled with rage. "Are you insane? We're going after them because our funds are running low. Where are you going to get money to—"

"They'll only get paid if they take the ship down," Zinqued broke in, but Paun wasn't convinced in the slightest.

"No one's going to take on that ship without a deposit," he said. "You do something like this again, and you're fired."

He walked away, determined to have the last word, but Zinqued called after him: "If I find the mercenaries to do the work for ten percent of the take, will you do it?" It was an audacious plan, but he really had nothing to lose. Even when Paun turned to him with a weary look, Zinqued did not waver.

"Yeah, sure." Paun looked at Zinqued like he was a toddler throwing a tantrum. "If you find some crews to do that, you let me know." He walked away shaking his head. He thought there was about as much chance of that, as finding out that stars came with on-off switches.

Zinqued, not deterred by his attitude, gave a triumphant look at Chofal. "I'm going to go send some messages."

"Zinqued." She sank her face into her hands. "You're getting obsessed. Paun's right; no one will want to do this for that small a share of the take."

Did you *hear* what happened at Virtue Station?" Zinqued asked. "He killed a bunch of the bankers' guards. I'm betting we can get some people who want the *Shinigami* taken down."

It would be easy enough, after all, to turn the crew members over to Virtue Station's justice and pretend the *Shinigami* had been damaged beyond repair in the fight.

He could do this. For this payout, he'd find a way to pull it off.

A message bleeped on the screen, and Uleq leaned forward to peer at it. His eyebrows went up, and he settled in to send a response.

Crallus watched him. Reading the Torcellan's thoughts was impossible. Was he pleased by the message he'd received, or was he angry? Was he responding favorably to someone, or threatening to kill them? His expression betrayed nothing.

Crallus reflected once again that he should probably not be Uleq's ally.

Uleq looked up and smiled. "It turns out someone else is hoping to deal with the *Shinigami*."

"Who?" Crallus wasn't surprised, only curious. Someone who tried to impose laws and Justice on the outer sectors, like Barnabas, was bound to accrue enemies.

"A petty ship thief." Uleq looked amused. "They sent a

message looking for mercenaries, and *I* have alerts set up in all of the major communication systems for people talking about the *Shinigami* or any other human ships. I was able to contact them before anyone else could."

"They're never going to—"

Uleq gave a careless shrug. "They've had a few run-ins with the ship and come away alive, and they have a plan. I'll give them some funding and see if they can capture the ship. I even have a plan for where, exactly, they can take it on." His face darkened. "We'll see what my sister thinks."

The words were bitter, and Crallus remembered with a chill that Ilia Yennai had not been pleased with Uleq.

He wondered just what they would walk into when they got to the Yennai Corporation headquarters.

"Five minutes." Zinqued slammed the message printout down on the table. "It took five minutes to find someone."

The crew members looked at one another silently, and Paun stared at Zinqued rather than the message.

"I assume this is some acceptance from a mercenary group, then?" Paun sounded unimpressed.

Zinqued ground his teeth. Paun would know exactly what this was if he had read it. "We're funded. In full. For as many mercenaries as we need."

"Who the hell would do that?" Paun frowned.

"Uleq Yennai. Apparently, the humans have caused them some problems."

"The Yennai Corporation?" Paun's face went stony.

"Once they have that ship in their grasp, they'll never give it up."

"Maybe." Though he had some plans on that score, he wasn't about to share them with Paun. "And maybe they'll be really grateful that someone took care of this for them."

Paun wavered, but then he looked around at the crew. All of them looked back, unimpressed. It had been a long few weeks without a job.

Without any bonuses.

"Fine," Paun acquiesced. He looked at all of them. "But I have a bad feeling about this." He stomped out of the room without looking back.

Zinqued smiled.

They'd see who the captain was when all of this was over.

The Yennai Corporation headquarters looked like nothing —a hunk of rock floating in outer space. There were no noticeable patrols, no buildings or visible entrances, and no emissions on any of the scanners.

"Are you sure this is the right place?" Crallus asked. He had a sudden vision of Ilia plunging their ship into the side of an asteroid.

"Yes," was all Uleq said. Despite his usual arrogant expression, he seemed ill at ease. He had grown more and more withdrawn as the ship came closer to its destination.

Crallus closed his eyes briefly and prayed that they weren't about to be executed.

There was a tiny, almost invisible, entrance covered by

a force field in the asteroid. The ship slid through and set down in an eerily empty landing bay, piloting itself the whole way. Uleq strode off of it with his face tight and angry. It didn't take any schooling in family politics to know that this was the worst kind of insult for him. They were humiliating him on purpose.

For the first time, Crallus felt *sorry* for Uleq.

He didn't say that, though. He knew enough about the guy to know that Uleq would probably murder him if he did.

They crossed the floor with their every movement echoing in the huge space, and Crallus' worry grew with each step. When the soldiers appeared, it was almost a relief. At least something was happening.

Uleq stopped, raising an eyebrow. "I take it my sister would like me to see her immediately."

The guard captain inclined his head. "In the Overlook, sir."

Uleq tensed, and his face went entirely flat. He did not look at Crallus, only set off with his footsteps moving quickly. Whatever was going to happen, he seemed to want it to be over with.

The Overlook appeared to be nothing more than another cavernous room, though there was a strange, bluish glow around the back of it. Uleq frowned as they were marched across the floor toward a single figure in white robes.

Ilia Yennai regarded them as they approached. Crallus could see the similarities between her and Uleq.

"Ilia," Uleq said shortly with a look of contempt.

"Uleq." The soldiers fanned out around her, and Ilia

didn't even give them a glance as she let loose on Uleq. "You have disgraced us. You have squandered resources on a useless vendetta."

"I have devoted every resource I have to our family's greatest enemy," Uleq shot back. "With your backing, we could have destroyed them by now. Instead, you have divided us, and our enemy has grown stronger."

She snorted. "The humans and their federation are no threat, brother. We will infiltrate them as we have infiltrated all other governments, and we will control them from the shadows. Had you served our interests, you would have spent your time on *that*."

"You have no idea what you are dealing with," Uleq retorted, his voice beginning to rise. "They will destroy us. They will—"

"I am not interested in hearing all of this again." Ilia shook her head, bored and elegant. "You will remain here until I decide what to do with you."

"Don't you mean, until Father decides what to do with me?" Uleq's challenge was delivered with narrowed eyes.

"Oh, no." Ilia's smile was supremely self-satisfied. "He's given me complete control in this matter."

She took a moment to savor the look on Uleq's face then swept out of the room with the soldiers surrounding her.

Uleq stood frozen, his eyes wide and horrified. Crallus watched him a moment then went to look at the glow at the edge of the room. The ground fell away sharply a few feet before the wall, and he looked down to see...

He froze.

"The radiation can't reach us." Uleq's voice made

Crallus jump. He nearly lost his footing and stumbled back from the edge, cursing, his heart pounding. Uleq peered over the edge with a strange detachment. "You see the force field? It keeps the radiation in. A modified version of what's at the end of our landing bays."

"Oh." Crallus nodded. He felt like an idiot.

"It doesn't stop a falling body, though." Finally, a trace of fear showed in Uleq's eyes. "This is where they hold executions."

17

The mercenaries met them on Tretoar, a station jumbled together from an old mining rig and a few cargo ships. Paun hated this place, though it was one of the best spots in the sector to offload stolen goods with no questions asked. The station managers there were some of the best paid in known space. Their cut was high, and for good reason: they never, ever gave information about who had gone through Tretoar.

Since Zinqued wasn't paying the station fee, he was happy to be using this place. Among other things, it showed that Uleq Yennai was serious.

Which was good, because, after a flurry of initial details, Uleq seemed to have dropped off the map.

All his money had cleared, though, and the mercenaries were eager to bargain for as much more as they could. As far as Zinqued could tell, he'd been given a blank check to hire as many as he wanted.

He stared out over the sea of mercenaries, all milling around between the ten ships, and considered.

Ten was a good number...for any other ship than this one.

"How many more ships can you bring?" he asked brusquely.

The syndicate leader, a grizzled old Shrillexian with one eye missing, gave Zinqued a small smile. "How many do you need?"

"Four times as many as this," Zinqued said promptly.

He had the satisfaction, at least, of seeing the old mercenary look taken aback. Then his face set as if he thought Zinqued didn't know what he was talking about. "I can get you ten more," the male said. He shrugged. "They're all good ships."

Zinqed only shrugged. "It's not *my* life on the line. I suppose we can try throwing twenty at it and see what happens. We'll just use more next time. And you might do some damage, after all."

The mercenary and Zinqued stared at each other for a long moment.

"I'll find you forty more," the mercenary said finally.

"Good," Zinqued said. He considered, then made his play, strolling away from Paun and motioning for the mercenary to follow him. "I have a buyer lined up for something on the ship," he said. "An object of sentimental value—he's an antiquities collector. You'll no doubt have been told to hand the ship over to the Yennai Corporation, hmm?"

The mercenary nodded impassively.

Zinqued smiled. "The amount of money he's willing to pay for this artifact is quite impressive. I assure you, and I do not say this lightly, that I can give you more than the

Yennai Corporation for your help in keeping the ship with me." He gave the other Shrillexian a look. "Remember, after all, that they would have sent you woefully underprepared. I am the one who is giving you a chance at survival."

The mercenary smiled at this and reached out one hand. "Pleasure doing business with you."

"And you." Zinqued nodded and headed back to Paun.

The mercenaries, after all, didn't need to know exactly what on the ship Zinqued wanted to sell. He wasn't about to dangle the exact payout under their noses just so they could steal it for themselves.

But he *would* reward them for their help. He'd decided that he would certainly be a benevolent leader.

Because after this, he would certainly have his own ship.

"Now, remember," Barnabas said. He checked the fit of his gauntlets and looked at Gar. "Don't let anyone get under your skin."

Gar nodded. Barnabas was smiling, but Gar knew he was absolutely serious about this.

"It wasn't...," he considered. "I didn't mean for things to get out of hand on Virtue Station. I'm sorry I lost my temper."

"Mmm." Barnabas slid on his holster. "Note that I didn't say, 'don't lose your temper.' I said, 'don't let anyone get under your skin.' There's a small but important difference."

Gar frowned. "I'm not sure I get it."

"Oh, it's very simple." Shinigami appeared, her avatar

projected on top of one of the weapons lockers. She sat cross-legged, watching them with a grin. "See, he loses his temper all the time, so he's not going to say you can't do *that*."

Barnabas gave her a look. "I do not lose my temper *all* the time. I lose my temper when the situation warrants it. Which is when someone has done something unjust, to hurt others. Me losing my temper is not the outcome they hope for in that case."

Shinigami considered this.

"Are you sure…" she asked finally, "that's not bullshit?"

Gar turned his snort of laughter into a cough and made himself very busy with his boots as Barnabas glared at Shinigami.

"Name one time when we've worked together that me losing my temper has been to our detriment," he said stiffly.

"To our *detriment*, ooh, how fancy." She hunched her shoulders with a grin. "You get so gentlemanly when you're upset."

Barnabas stopped talking entirely and devoted himself to his armor, with the air of someone who is not going to deign to join the conversation. Shinigami snickered, and Gar tried to decide if he should move unobtrusively to the nearest blast door in case of a fight.

It was a welcome distraction when Jeltor appeared with an obviously distressed Tafa at his side.

"I'm coming in with you," the Jotun announced. "Out into the compound, I mean."

Barnabas looked up in surprise. "You should not feel obligated," he said politely. "I regret that we are bringing you with us. It is simply that time is of the essence. You have helped by giving us information. We do not need anything further, I assure you."

"See?" Tafa demanded of Jeltor. "He also thinks you shouldn't do this."

"I would *like* to come," Jeltor said patiently. To Tafa, he added, "Your concern is touching, but I will be quite safe."

"How?" Shinigami asked practically. "Don't get me wrong, your suit is impressive, but the Jotun fleet has never had an infantry engagement. Unless you're trained for combat—"

They broke off as Jeltor activated his suit. The hands slid back to be replaced with double-barreled guns, one bayonetted. Pieces of the suit hummed with an electrical charge, a plate came down over the capsule that held Jeltor's body, and the suit seemed to sink down into a mechanical version of a warrior's crouch. To top it off, a panel slid to uncover a long, thin arm in the suit's chest, with a hacking-tip at the end.

"I am trained for combat," Jeltor said, amused.

Barnabas laughed delightedly, his good mood entirely restored. "Well, then," he said. "We would be glad to have you along."

"Only if you don't intend to do something stupidly heroic," Shinigami said. "I'd hate for you to die before I could get a better look at that suit."

Jeltor laughed, not at all offended by her focus. "It's made to…shall we say, confuse scanners."

"Yeah, I didn't see *any* of that." She was so intrigued that it took a moment before she added to Barnabas, "Sorry."

"No apologies necessary." Barnabas smiled at Jeltor. "I

sense the Jotun and the Federation might have quite a happy partnership, should they choose to make the trade," he considered. "And Jean Dukes would probably enjoy a chat with some of your engineers."

"I would be pleased to meet your Jean Dukes," Jeltor acknowledged politely. "There are many pieces of your technology that we have heard of and believed to be exaggerations...until I came to be on this ship. Now I am beginning to think the stories were true. It is...worrisome."

"Unless the Jotun Navy goes around enslaving people, or otherwise perpetrating mass injustice, I don't think we'll have a problem."

Barnabas and Shinigami had spent part of the previous night going over what they could find of Jotun history and military engagements. They had found one recurring piece of advice from a variety of sources and phrased in a variety of ways, but all boiled down to the same thing—don't fuck with the Jotun people, and you won't get massacred. They didn't deploy their military often, but when they did...it was with extremely impressive results.

Barnabas and Shinigami had decided they both liked what they saw.

Tafa, however, still looked worried. "But what if you all get hurt?" Even a week ago she would have said that Jeltor infuriated her—and she hadn't known Gar, Barnabas, or Shinigami. Now, however, she knew she would be devastated if any of them were to die.

"We will not take unnecessary risks," Barnabas promised her. "*Will we?*" he added meaningfully, looking around at the rest of the group. Grumbles were his only response, and he smiled at Tafa. "See? We'll be quite all right."

"If you say so." Tafa hunched her shoulders. "I just feel like this is a bit too easy. There has to be some sort of trap."

"There usually is," Barnabas agreed cheerfully. "Luckily for us, Shinigami is sneakier than almost anyone."

"So are you," Shinigami shot back pointedly. "In any event, we're coming up on the base if anyone wants to get a look."

Vedoon was bored.

When he'd been hired by the Yennai corporation, he'd been sure that his life would be filled with plenty of action. After all, no one got that big and powerful without plenty of soldiers, right?

Then he'd gotten stationed *here*, of all places.

Nothing ever happened here.

Vedoon sighed as he looked out at the ramparts and grounds. As far as he knew, the Yennai family had never even been here. Some big, secret headquarters this had proved to be. He'd thought there would be secret meetings, with him standing proudly outside the door in his armor, close to the seat of power.

They said Ilia Yennai wasn't bad looking, either...

But he'd never seen her. She'd never come here. There was a small army of guards stationed here, and a ridiculous amount of gun turrets and munitions, but there was never anyone important.

How was a guard supposed to rise in the hierarchy if

NATALIE GREY & MICHAEL ANDERLE

there weren't any higher-ups to impress? He'd had a plan—distinguish himself in training, get nominated as a personal bodyguard for one of the Yennai family, and make his fortune. Seducing Ilia had been one of those ideas he didn't pin too much on. She probably had some rich husband. A guard could dream, though.

He'd just leaned on the balustrade next to his patrol partner when they heard the boom of a ship entering the atmosphere. The turrets nearby blazed to life before they even had time to wonder if this was a Yennai ship. A moment later, the klaxons blared.

They were under attack. A rush of adrenaline hit Vedoon, and he gave a whoop.

Finally, he was going to have a chance to distinguish himself.

"Ms. Yennai."

"What?" After her brother's nonsense, Ilia was in no mood for more bad news—and she sensed from her servant's tone that this message was bad news.

"A human ship has attacked the decoy base. The name is *Shinigami*. They've taken out several of the turrets in their initial pass and don't appear to be damaged."

Ilia turned slowly. "*Shinigami*?"

"Yes, ma'am."

Ilia's mind raced. Was it possible that Uleq had been right? If he was, what would her father say?

Her lips curved in a smile. Her father would be pleased with *her*, not Uleq. Because she would be the one who took the *Shinigami* down and eliminated the threat. After all, Uleq was locked in the Overlook.

He couldn't interfere.

She realized the guard was still staring at her. "You may go," she said simply. She swept to her chair as he left, stretching her hands along the arms. Someday soon, she would be in her father's office, in the high-backed chair that held controls for all the Yennai Corporation's fleets.

For so long, she had been the favored child, and she basked in his approval.

However, lately, she wondered if she might hasten things along. Her father'd had had a good life, after all.

And it was time for her to take her place at the head of the corporation. She would take out this human ship, then she would decide on her next course of action. She considered, then rang a bell. The servant appeared again, looking worried.

"Take my brother's communication devices and scan the ship he came in and the one he used to get to Virtue Station," Ilia instructed. "I want all communications brought to me."

18

"This place is nice," Barnabas said appreciatively.

Shinigami and Gar both gave him a look. The ship presently weaved through a veritable hail of projectiles and pulse weaponry, and preliminary scans showed that the building was rife with soldiers and larger cannons that were being manned and warmed up.

"Not the turrets *specifically*," Barnabas said, rolling his eyes. "It's just a nice building. Nice planet, too. Atmosphere?"

"Totally toxic to most life forms," Shinigami reported. She paused for a moment, and there was the distant shudder of missiles launching. She brought their path up on screen before she continued. "One of the Yennai Corporation's biggest technological breakthroughs is something they haven't sold at all—it's a type of force field they can modify at will. It can distinguish between different gases and keep them separate, which is what it's doing around the palace. It can trap radiation, all sorts of things. They'd make a fortune selling the schematics, or even manufacturing it, but they've just kept it for themselves."

"I can't blame them." Barnabas settled back in his chair. "When you've got good technology and a lot of enemies, you don't advertise what you're capable of." He gave a grim smile. "Unfortunately for them, we're rather farther ahead than most adversaries they're facing, technologically speaking."

"Is that your fancy, old-fashioned way of saying we're going to bend them over a table?"

"*Shinigami!* Gar, do *not* look that up." Barnabas pressed a hand over his eyes. "Where on Earth— You know, never mind."

"Tabitha and Pete were—"

"I said I didn't want to know!" Barnabas looked at the door into the rest of the ship. "It's a pity I can't get drunk anymore. I'd like to have a very large drink right now."

Shinigami was still laughing when her missiles made impact. Of the seventy-four missile turrets, she'd found so far, she had taken out eighteen. She'd like to take out more, ostensibly because it would be better to get these taken care of before the larger cannons came online. In reality, it was because she liked to blow things up, and turrets full of ammunition blew up *very* nicely.

The avatar turned suddenly to the door. "Jeltor is asking permission to come onto the bridge."

"Let him in." Barnabas looked curious. He nodded to Jeltor as the Jotun came through the doors. "Jeltor. What can I do for you?"

"Believe me, I would not interrupt a battle to ask for a

favor." Jeltor sounded amused. "Though this is a far more… quiet battle than most I have been a part of."

"Mmm." Barnabas nodded to Shinigami's avatar. "That is due to our pilot and gunner."

"Finally, I get the respect I deserve," Shinigami said, in a long-suffering tone.

Barnabas shook his head slightly. He looked at Jeltor.

"I have received more information," Jeltor explained. "Some schematics came through. They're of anti-aircraft systems this base has in place, as well as our estimate of the optimal targets to take out to create dead zones."

Shinigami looked at him through narrowed eyes.

"She prefers to blow up *everything*," Barnabas clarified gravely.

"I'll at least *look*." Shinigami gestured for Jeltor to bring up the displays.

"You see here," the Jotun said, pointing to a series of large cannons that were embedded in the walls near the center of the large compound. "These are shrapnel cannons. They're becoming quite popular. They were invented by the Boreir Group."

"You won't be seeing many more of them then," Barnabas murmured.

Shinigami snickered. She lit up the diagrams. "So, you want us to take out those six and land…where?"

"Here." Jeltor walked over to the screen and pointed.

"Good call." Shinigami nodded. She looked at Barnabas. "Agreed, Chief?"

Barnabas stared at the diagram with a slight frown on his face. He tapped his fingers on the arm of the chair for a moment.

"What if you took out *this* configuration?" He walked up to the screen and tapped on certain guns. Shinigami lit them up as he tapped, and a green overlay appeared to show the safe zone. He was smiling. "It works. Do that."

"But that doesn't make any sense," Jeltor pointed out slowly. "With all due respect," he added to Barnabas hastily.

"He's right," Shinigami added. "When you get to the top of the green zone, where are you going?"

Barnabas' smile grew. He waited, arms crossed until Shinigami's mouth opened in a little O of surprise.

"Ohhhh," she said. "Oh, you sneaky bastard. I love it."

"What?" Jeltor looked back and forth between them. "What are you planning?"

"You'll see," Barnabas and Shinigami said at the same time.

The compound was in chaos. Vedoon ducked under an ornamental arch and sprinted for the end of the courtyard. This place had been well-made, alright, just as functional as it was beautiful. When the proximity alerts went off, the shrapnel cannons embedded in the ground had sprung up and begun to arm. They needed soldiers to help with targeting and final authorization, but they could do most everything on their own.

Of course, most of them now had broken fountains on top. The place hadn't been designed for *multiple* attacks.

Also, it was ridiculous to have a battle in a garden.

A missile hit the nearest cannon and blew Vedoon off his feet. He tumbled, feeling a few pieces of shrapnel hit his armor, then got up and ran. His helmet had cushioned the fall, so he didn't need to worry about a concussion.

"Get away from the cannons!" His squad leader grabbed Vedoon's arm.

"No! We have to get them all online!"

"They're taking them all out!" Lolori was insistent. "Vedoon!"

Vedoon stopped, torn. Running for the shelters was the smart thing to do. There was a line of shattered cannons that proved Lolori right.

And yet...this was his chance to distinguish himself.

Their opponent made the decision for him. A missile struck one of the cannons up ahead, and the barrel flew off to strike an ornamental column. Vedoon tackled Lolori out of the way as chunks of stone and shrapnel from the cannon's reserves rained down on them.

When Vedoon picked his head up, he thought Lolori was dead at first. The squad leader stared up with a look of horror on his face. Then he gulped slightly and pointed, and Vedoon turned to look.

"Oh, no," he whispered.

The compound had been cunningly set up. There was a main portion with a high, golden dome and plenty of pleasure gardens. There was even a big audience hall for all the functions and parties that never happened here—Vedoon was still a little annoyed about that. It was made, in short, to look like the most important part of the building. There was even a tower that looked like it probably held the apartments for the Yennai family.

But none of the *important* things were in that building. Instead, they lay in one of the three smaller outbuildings.

The family's apartments were located below ground, with a series of mirrored passageways to fill them with sunlight. There were reserves of food and water.

The tower that resembled a scanner tower held the family's offices and conference chambers.

No one should know that. No one should have been able to figure out the layout of this place.

Then again, no one should have been able to find them in the first place.

But that damned ship hovered in the air beside the tower. It had taken out any cannons that could reach that part of the building, and there was no one to stop the people inside from doing…

What *were* they planning to do?

Vedoon didn't know. All he knew was that they had to get there and stop these people.

"Come on." He hauled Lolori up. "Call as many people as you can. We have to get to that tower!"

"No distress signals," Shinigami reported. She had given her avatar a cape again, and it whipped in the wind from the open shuttle bay door. It was a nice touch, though Barnabas thought she'd look even more impressive if the cloak hung still, like a single figure untroubled by a hurricane.

"To whom would they send a distress signal?" He asked reasonably. "They have a damned army here already." He spoke into the comm unit in his helmet.

Nearby, Jeltor fed codes to one of the outside windows

to crack it open without them resorting to laser-cutting or missiles. Shinigami had been very put out by that but was appeased when Barnabas suggested that any servers that *weren't* destroyed would be filled with data and schematics for her to play with.

Right now, however, she was frowning. "I don't like it," she insisted. "Tafa said this was a trap, and she definitely knows—being part of a family of assholes, right?"

Barnabas snorted with amusement at that. Jeltor shouted and waved when the window popped open.

"Keep scanning," Barnabas told Shinigami. "If you see anything dangerous, we'll get out of there. Until then… we'll proceed as if these people had no idea their base could be overrun, and they're going to be judged and executed." He smiled and nodded to her.

As he ran and jumped across the gap, he could feel the familiar anticipation of a mission. These were very bad people. They were a source of evil and oppression in the quadrant. Once Barnabas brought them to Justice, the quadrant could go on as it was meant to.

He landed and rolled, with Gar and Jeltor right behind him. Jeltor had some combination of grav technology and a bunch of spring-loaded devices that helped launch him across the gap and balanced him as he did so. He landed with only the faintest squeak of metal and ducked the top of his suit in a nod to Barnabas.

"Where *is* everyone?" Gar asked.

There was a pause while they all looked at each other. Then Barnabas sprinted for the main room.

When he got there, he cursed. It wasn't filled with booby-traps. No, everything about this place from the grounds to the barracks was maintained. They had probably kept it here just in case they needed it.

But this was definitely a gigantic decoy.

"Son of a traitorous whore," Barnabas murmured.

You should get more creative with your swearing. "Son of a donkey-balled ass muncher," for instance.

I'll keep that in mind, thank you. Barnabas sank down to a crouch, considering. *So what do we do now?*

Well, I doubt we'll find anything, but definitely, do see if you can get to any computers. And in the meantime, you have a few dozen soldiers headed your way.

And what do we do about that?

I was thinking—maybe a variant on one of our signature moves. Give me a few, and I'll let you know if I can pull it off.

Barnabas smiled and went to find the servers.

19

Crallus had begun his career as a mercenary, and a damned good one. He killed with brutal efficiency, and he was known for his vigilance. He didn't relax when on a job—*ever.*

So for the first few hours of their imprisonment on the Overlook, he paced and listened for the footsteps outside the door. He learned that patrols went by more or less every hour, though he was not yet sure if the variation was for the purposes of security, or due to laziness. He hadn't seen them fight so he couldn't make a good assessment of their character yet.

Yes, they'd looked very impressive, all fanned out around Ilia—but anyone could stand still and glower at people for a few minutes.

His mind filled with plans as he paced. If they came in for execution with anything less than ten guards, Crallus was fairly sure he stood a chance of escaping.

There was the Overlook, of course, which was just as much a danger to them as it was to him. He could surround himself with guards, since they wouldn't want to shoot into the group. Or there was the fact that they wore plate armor, and he could sink his claws into the gaps.

Plus, he'd marked the route from the landing bay and had taken note of which doors had the green light to indicate a ship on the pad. If he could break free, he might be able to get to a ship and get away.

Uleq probably wouldn't make it.

Crallus wasn't sure how he felt about that. More accurately, he felt guilty about it, and he disliked the guilt. Uleq had gotten him into this mess, and there was no reason that Crallus should have to die just because he'd met Uleq Yennai first, instead of Ilia Yennai.

Uleq would die, that was just the way it was. He wasn't the heir to the Yennai Corporation, and he made no secret about not accepting that. Ilia would have to be an idiot to let him live, and she wasn't an idiot.

So he was going to die. Really, the only question was whether Crallus could survive.

But he felt guilty leaving Uleq to face execution alone. His father had left him to Ilia's mercy, and surely the Torcellan patriarch knew what that meant.

Crallus clenched his hand and hissed a long breath out.

"Stop *pacing*," Uleq said coldly from the side of the room. He had taken a seat on a stone bench that had been carved roughly out of the wall. *We're not getting out,* his tone said. He wanted to be comfortable before he died. He had given up.

And it was clear that he hadn't even considered trying to bargain for Crallus' life.

All sympathy vanished. Crallus gave Uleq a long, hard

look and went to sit, his mind pivoting in a different direction.

Namely, was Ilia Yennai looking for any new employees?

As if summoned by some otherworldly force, Ilia strode into the room. She had changed her robes to a deep purple, and she looked absolutely furious.

"How could you?" she demanded of Uleq, without even a pause for breath.

Uleq looked up with a sardonic smile. He expected this altercation, clearly. "Dear sister, let us dispense with all of this." He kept his elbows resting on his knees. "Are you putting on a show for Father, pretending to look over my crimes and reach an opinion on whether or not you should execute me? Are you pretending to struggle over that possibility? We both know you'll kill me eventually. Put on whatever act you like for Father, but do not make me play along." He settled back, finally, and pulled his hood up so that his face was shrouded. With his arms crossed over his chest, he gave every indication that he was going to sleep.

Ilia, however, was not prepared to give up so easily.

"I've never pretended," she hissed. "For years, I've antic-ipated the day I could have you killed. I never liked you. I never trusted you."

Uleq didn't move at all, and Crallus decided that the best thing to do would be to pretend to be a statue. He sat as still as possible and hoped Ilia wouldn't notice him.

He'd be better off not serving her, either, he decided. This whole family was fucking crazy.

Ilia paced, shooting regular glances at Uleq. "I would

have killed you even if you'd come back here and been the good little brother. We both know that."

Although Uleq didn't move, he chuckled from inside the hood. "Yes. We do."

"So did you *have* to destroy the better part of a hundred ships in the meantime?" Ilia snarled. "What were you hoping to do? Destroy my legacy just for spite?"

"Surprisingly, no." Uleq's breath stirred the hood, but otherwise, he was motionless. "Your guess only makes sense if I were resigned to my fate. Which I was not."

"Then *why*?" Ilia's hands clenched next to her head as if she would tear at her hair. "We had word that Get'ruz Shipping was entirely destroyed in an engagement, but only now do we learn it was an engagement *you* sent them to. And Syndicate Yerr? What about them? We hear that their base has been destroyed."

Crallus tried to blend into the background. Ilia didn't appear to notice that the syndicate leader was sitting right in front of her, and he didn't have any particular desire to get involved in this fight.

Uleq said nothing to this.

"*Why*?" Ilia screamed. Her voice was raw.

"*Why*?" Uleq pushed the hood back, and his face was flushed with fury. He shoved himself up. "Why? You *dare* ask that of me? I've told you a hundred times why. Because *one ship* was able to take them out. That's how powerful the humans are. *That's* why they need to be destroyed."

"That's why we can't take them on!" Ilia yelled. "We don't fight battles in fleets, not yet. We control from the shadows. We would have infiltrated their federation and—"

"They would never have allowed that," Uleq voiced

contemptuously. His tone dripped with hatred. "They have *morals.*"

"People who plead *morals* are just holding out for the right bribe," Ilia snapped. She crossed her arms over her chest.

"Not. These. Aliens." Uleq spat each word out. "They don't allow just anyone into their upper ranks. They watch. They don't take bribes. They don't *want* money. They want to rule the universe. They want everyone to follow their Queen's ways." He pressed his advantage. "They would have found us, and they would have destroyed us. If you had mobilized all our resources against them when we first saw them like I told you to do when they were already engaged with other wars—"

"You really believe they can't be bribed?"

Uleq gave a wordless yell of fury. "No! They can't!"

Ilia raised an eyebrow. "Then they can be defeated by other means. We *have* a fleet."

"You need to get into their systems!" Uleq yelled. His voice was hoarse with rage. "You need their AI, you need what's on the ship I was following. I wasn't trying to destroy this, Ilia, I was trying to *save* it!"

Ilia stared at him for a long moment then her lip curled. "You still don't understand, do you?"

She swept away for the door, and Uleq stared after her in disbelief. "I don't understand? *I* don't understand?"

She paused in the doorway. "No," she said sweetly. "You don't." She slipped out, and Uleq flung himself at the door with a roar of fury, beating at it with his fist.

"I'll fucking kill you!" he screamed. "You're destroying

us! I'll make sure you die. Even if you kill me, Father will know soon enough that you—"

The door reverberated with a hollow BOOM as if struck from the other side, and Uleq was flung away from it to slide across the rocky floor.

He picked himself up. He did not look at Crallus. The mercenary leader was suddenly sure Uleq did not remember he was here at all.

"You've destroyed us," Uleq whispered. "You stupid bitch."

Out in the hallway, Ilia watched as the guard slammed a special mace against the door. The security cameras showed Uleq sliding back across the floor and carried his words to her clearly.

She smiled coldly.

If she wanted to defeat this human ship, she had to know his plan—but he would never have told her if she'd simply asked. So she had to use his greatest weakness against him.

It was very simple. Uleq had to be the smartest person in the room. No matter how clever his plan was or *would* be if he didn't spill it to everyone, he couldn't resist the urge to explain it so that people could be astounded by his genius.

"Who's the real genius, Uleq?" Ilia narrowed her eyes. "The person who comes up with the plans and does all the research...or the person who lets other people do the work for her, and takes the credit?"

She gave a cold smile and walked away, pleased.

She'd been in contact with the ship thieves Uleq had hired. With their mercenaries, they were well-placed to take out a single ship, particularly if it was grounded at the base. Uleq's plan had been a sound one, now that she understood why he'd made it the way he had. He wanted the AI core from that ship.

Soon she would have it, and *she* would decide what to do with it.

Because Ilia had her plan. When this mission was done, her father would come to congratulate her on a job well done. He would want to see the AI core in action, after all. She would bask in his approval and let everyone see how he loved her, and what a good heir she was. They would execute Uleq together so there would be no challenge from that quarter.

Then her father would have an accident.

Ilia's smile grew. She had lived her life fearing that someone would find this base and attack it. Now, she welcomed it. Power would be within her grasp in only a few days, and she could hardly wait.

The battering ram swung forward, and the big double doors to the tower shuddered.

"Again!" Vedoon yelled. At the front of the battering ram, his hands aching and sweat running into his eyes, he reflected that he had never felt more alive. This was exhilarating. The door would be down soon, and they could take their revenge on the intruders.

He heaved the battering ram forward and welcomed the jolt of pain that shuddered through his body as the ram hit. The soldiers behind him gave a cheer. They could sense that victory was close.

Then the lights flickered, and a female voice came over the speakers.

"Hello, soldiers of the Yennai Corporation."

The soldiers paused, and Vedoon wondered what to do. Was this a distraction? Should they keep fighting?

"I am Shinigami," the voice said. "You do not know me, but I have witnessed many battles in my time, and your valor today has not gone unnoticed."

The soldiers murmured to one another, and Vedoon felt his chest puff up in pride. Then he wondered what this Shinigami character wanted. Had she hoped they would defect?

He would never defect. Not when everything he had dreamed of was within his grasp.

"No doubt you will be wondering where your rein-forcements are," Shinigami told them. "The truth is, none are coming. You see, this is a decoy base. The Yennai family has never come here and never intended to do so. They left a trail to this base so that if anyone ever came for them—and they have many enemies, all well-earned, I assure you—this decoy base would be destroyed. They hoped, no doubt, that it would be destroyed by bombardment so that no one would ever realize they had escaped."

There was a pause.

"As you have doubtless realized, this means that all of you were intended as nothing more than a sacrifice. Your valor, as you fought for the defense of the base, would convince many opponents that this was no decoy."

Vedoon felt his stomach drop. He had assumed that the Yennai family simply traveled a lot and were too busy to come back here. But the fact that they had *never* been here…

Yes, it all fit.

He looked at the other soldiers and found the same betrayal in their faces.

"Rest assured that we have no quarrel with you," Shinigami said. "We have an offer, in fact. Certain reserves of cash exist on this base. It was *your* home, and the Yennai Corporation undoubtedly owes you a debt. Therefore, we propose the following: if you tell us what you know, any fact that might lead us to the true base, the money will be split amongst all of you and the ships will be unlocked to give you safe passage to wherever you would like to go. You may discuss this offer amongst yourselves."

20

"They're ready to talk," Shinigami reported.

Barnabas, seated at the head of the conference table in the main Yennai offices, looked up curiously. "Any idea of their intentions?"

"They're all laying down their weapons, and from what I've been able to pick out on the voice scanners—not as much as I'd hoped, they weren't made for a lot of voices at once—they want to take the offer. Only one or two are looking shifty."

"I can deal with one or two," Barnabas said in satisfaction. He smiled at Gar and Jeltor. "This really is our best trick."

"I'm not sure it qualifies as a *trick*," Jeltor said. "Unless you don't actually give them the money."

Barnabas looked horrified. "We do give them the money! And they usually don't deserve to die." He gave a small shrug. "That said, should any of their thoughts show a particular need for Justice…"

"What else are we here for, after all?" Shinigami asked prosaically. "Should I open the doors?"

"Yes, please." Barnabas gestured to Gar and Jeltor. It wasn't for effect, but shelter. The chair was bulletproof, so if anyone here started shooting, they could duck while Barnabas killed the would-be assassin.

When the doors opened, only a few aliens came into the room. Barnabas recognized them from the security tapes. One was a Leath, which surprised him.

Shinigami, anything shady with the Leath?

Surprisingly, not that I can tell. No suicide vest or anything. I guess you're looking at someone like Gar—he left his home planet behind because he didn't live that life.

Ah. Well, keep an eye on him. Barnabas nodded courteously to the Leath. "I am Barnabas. You are?"

"Lolori," the Leath said. He nodded. "I think I saw some worry in your eyes. Believe me when I say that I bear no ill will for what happened between our races. I only wish more could have seen the truth so that battle could be avoided entirely."

"Now that they have, do you not want to go back?" Barnabas asked curiously.

The Leath gave a thin smile. "No. It will take some time for the old ways to fade away completely, and I like the life I have found out here." He looked around at the other soldiers. "We have other things to discuss, however."

"That, we do." Barnabas nodded. He looked at a Shrillexian. "And you are?"

"Vedoon." The Shrillexian's voice grated somewhat, but he did not seem angry. He looked conflicted. "Do you swear this is no trick?"

"I swear," Barnabas assured. "You have been ill-treated by the Yennai Corporation. As far as I am concerned, the funds here rightly go to you more so than to any of their leaders."

"And if we do not have any useful information?" Vedoon asked.

"Ah. If I find out you have *withheld* information, I will be displeased. However, if you do not have it, I can hardly fault you for that. The deal is simply that what you have, I request you give to me."

"Why?" Lolori said now. "Why are you hunting them down?"

Barnabas smiled slightly. "What they did to you is not enough?"

The guards looked at one another and shrugged. Lolori answered for them all. "We are guards. We're here to be in danger, so they don't have to be. It was a trick, yes, and we do not like it...but it is the sort of thing we anticipated."

Barnabas had not considered that. His eyebrows rose as he absorbed this information.

"It's the way of the universe," Vedoon said, with another shrug. "People wouldn't hire guards otherwise, right?"

"Mmm." Barnabas tried to find a way to explain. "Say, rather, that this is a larger pattern of behavior. The Yennai Corporation made a great deal of money from theft and murder. They made allies of people who would steal ships or cargo, trade slaves, and sell munitions without any care for who bought them or how they would be used."

The guards still looked blank.

"You knew all of this, surely," Barnabas said.

"Yes, but…" Lolori cleared his throat and looked at the others. "Such things happen."

"You willingly live in a situation where your family might be enslaved or murdered, where the goods that supply your planet might be stolen, ruining your livelihood?" Barnabas frowned.

"Willingly?" Lolori laughed. "That is how things are. There are always those who do things like that. You kill them if you can when they come for you."

"What if you didn't have to?" Barnabas asked quietly. "What if that *wasn't* the way the universe worked?"

Their faces remained blank for a long moment. None of them had considered such a thing, that much was clear. Then they began to look hopeful…and then sad.

"We can't have that," Lolori insisted. "It doesn't exist. It never will."

"There will always be those who try to do such things," Barnabas agreed. "But there will also, always be those who hunt them. I am one of those people. I do it very well. And with the Federation, we have the chance to tip the balance. More people will be safe. More people will be strong enough to fight those who would hurt them.

"The Yennai Corporation profits off everything that hurts people, and they do it on purpose, for power. *That* is why I am going after them. They are evil. They hurt innocents. When they are gone, the universe will be that much safer."

The guards looked at one another one more time and seemed to come to a conclusion. Finally, Lolori nodded.

"I think they're somewhere near the Votayett system,"

he said. "I couldn't tell you where apart from that, but I'd been looking at the scrambling they used for their messages when they'd communicate with us. The same places would pop up over and over again. I think they'd send it through an exchange first so you could only trace it back so far, but for us, the message came through a relay on Seres."

That's the third planet in the Votayett system, Shinigami reported. *There's really nothing around there except those planets, but he's right that they probably wouldn't give anyone a direct link back to their base.*

We'll see what we can make of it, Barnabas told her.

To the soldiers, he nodded. "Thank you. Is there anything else?"

They shook their heads, and he felt their sincerity. He dismissed them to begin preparations for leaving. This base would be shuttered, and its location sent to Bethany Anne in case she wanted to establish an outpost.

If nothing else, she would likely want to send engineers to assess the various armaments and force field tech.

In truth, he wasn't upset with what they had learned. It had been unlikely in the extreme that any people as careful as the Yennai family would leave glaring clues or grant their expendable guards the location of the real base.

But, as in many cases, there were often small details that a clever person could put together, as Lolori had.

Barnabas led the way down the stairs to the ornamental gardens where *Shinigami* waited. While they were here— with the systems at their disposal, they'd try to narrow down that link to Seres.

The Yennai Corporation could only run for so long.

Zinqued dozed in his bunk when Paun came to get him.

"The client wants to talk to you." Paun's voice was tight with frustration, and Zinqued knew why. Paun was the captain. He should be the one people spoke to.

It filled Zinqued with glee. He agreed with Paun, after all. People *should* speak to the captain. To the person in charge. If he was the one they spoke to...

He gave a small smile as he got up and made his way to the bridge.

To his surprise, it was a Torcellan female that waited, not a male. He had thought Uleq was a male name. He frowned. "I am Zinqued."

"Zinqued." The female's voice was sweet. "I am Ilia Yennai. My brother, Uleq, assisted me in setting up this deal. As you know, the *Shinigami* is a dangerous ship, and he has had to take shelter from it. He was able to pass along your information, however, and we will complete this together."

Zinqued nodded and settled back in the chair. So that was why Uleq hadn't responded to messages.

"We are glad to be working with someone clever enough to have engaged with the *Shinigami* multiple times and yet emerge unscathed." Ilia smiled at Zinqued. "You will have to tell me how you managed that—after this is all over, of course."

Zinqued thought of the message they had received the last time—that they were too pathetic to even bother killing—and hoped he could come up with a good lie by the time they spoke.

He nodded, though. You didn't let your clients see your worry. "Of course, Ms. Yennai."

She smiled. "Due to your expertise, we will be increasing your pay for this mission, and I hope I will be able to present it to you personally."

"Of course," Zinqued agreed, smiling. It was well known that rich business owners sometimes liked to slum with hired hands, and he'd started to think he might receive a *very* warm welcome, indeed, from Ilia Yennai.

"I've transferred coordinates to your ship," Ilia shared. "You will rendezvous with our fleet there and be brought to our base."

Zinqued nodded.

"I look forward to meeting you," Ilia's pale mouth curved in a sweet smile and she ended the call.

Zinqued sat back in his chair, satisfied.

"This is going too well," Paun said from behind him.

Zinqued jumped and spun around in his chair. "Why are you here?"

"Because I'm the captain," Paun said. "And as the captain, I've made more deals than you have. I've learned how to tell when someone's about to stab me in the back. She's about to stab you in the back."

"No, she's not," Zinqued argued.

"Think what you want," Paun said. "You've clearly got the crew on your side. I just know that when we're at the base, I'm not going to be standing too close to you."

He left, shaking his head, with Zinqued staring after him.

Ilia opened a channel to her fleet captain. A Torcellan by the name of Wirav, he had been chosen by her father...who had added Ilia into the bargain as a wife. Uleq had already been married off for an alliance, leaving only one child to be sold.

Ilia was still bitter about it. She never liked speaking to Wirav or calling him her husband.

He knew it, too.

"Dearest wife," he said, as the channel opened.

"Husband." She gritted her teeth on the word but managed to get it out with a smile.

He arched one eyebrow. *Coming to terms with me?* His smile asked.

She ignored that. "There will be ships arriving shortly. I've sent the designations. They will need to have tracking disabled, and towed to the base."

"Are you sure that's necessary?"

"Yes," Ilia said simply. She would not let a random set of contractors know the location of the base...even if she intended to kill any survivors after the engagement. She did not believe in sloppy plans, and she felt no reason to explain this to Wirav, either. She waited, staring him down.

He shrugged as if it did not matter. "I will look forward to seeing you when I return."

"Indeed." Ilia smiled again.

"You do not hate me half so much as you claim," he said quietly, smiling. "Admit it, Ilia—you have liked having me for your husband."

She pretended to waver.

"I knew it." His smile grew. "I will see you soon, wife."

He ended the call, and the smile dropped off her face. Let Wirav think he had some hold on her.

He didn't, and when she got rid of her father, she would get rid of Wirav as well.

21

The message came in near the end of Fretor's shift, and he bobbed wearily in his tank as he opened it. When he saw who it was from, his surprise made the mechanical arms on his suit spasm. He spun in his tank, looking around for his captain.

"You! Recruit! Find the captain."

"Yes, sir." The new recruit hastened away, clanking down the corridors at high speed.

Fretor considered the message, and it wasn't long until the recruit came back with both the captain and one of the admirals, both on board right now for the ship's assessment near the Jotun capital planet.

"What's going on here?" the admiral demanded. "We have a very tight schedule."

The captain was not upset to be disturbed. He had worked with Fretor for many years and knew that he would not be summoned to the bridge during an important meeting unless there was ample cause. He nodded to

Fretor and had a much more pleasant tone as he said, "What is it, Fretor?"

"Sir, we've received a message from Jeltor."

"Jeltor!" The captain pulsed faintly blue in happiness and his body shook. "Is it an open call?"

"I'm afraid not, sir."

"I am glad he is well." The captain and Jeltor were old friends, having grown up together in the warm seas of the capital city. When Jeltor was captured while on a diplomatic mission, the captain had taken it hard.

"Yes. It seems he was rescued recently." Fretor looked at the message and worried slightly. If it were only the captain here things might be different, but with the *admiral...*

It was hard to know how this might go.

"He was in touch with Intelligence," the Admiral rumbled. As a high-ranking officer, he had a power suit that most Jotun would kill to own. It was a marvel of engineering, never squeaked, and it could plug into any ship and control it—even a carrier. There were rumors that he had personally directed the maneuvers and missiles of the JFS *Wallatar* during the battle of Hero's Gulf.

Fretor reminded himself to be respectful. After all, those Jotun who rose in the ranks were the ones with the mental capacity to control much at one time. The admiral was a war hero.

Which meant that his opinions on Jeltor's message would be important.

Fretor swallowed and directed his console to spin so that both the captain and the admiral could read it.

There was a long pause, then the admiral rumbled,

"He has *got* to be kidding."

Barnabas poked his head into one of the conference rooms, where Jeltor paced back and forth, the arms of his suit flailing in a show of agitation. He assessed Jeltor's thoughts, and after a moment Barnabas decided that this would be the equivalent of frowning and sighing for a human—not quite as dramatic as it would be if a human flailed their arms around.

He had to admit it was funny to watch, though.

"You've been shut in here for quite a while," he said.

Jeltor stopped pacing and looked at him. Both the suit and the jellyfish body seemed to swivel when he did that.

"You mean, I sent a message, and you don't know what was in it, and you're curious." He sounded amused by that, at least.

Barnabas leaned against the door frame, smiling. "Oh, we know what was in it."

Jeltor laughed at that. "You humans never cease to amaze me. I hope you will forgive my habit of sending encrypted messages."

"You're part of Jotun high command," Barnabas observed. "I'd be surprised if you didn't do that."

"Precisely. I am glad you see it that way." Jeltor swiveled his suit's body and nodded to one of the screens in the corner. "I am waiting for a response to my message to the fleet. I embedded a small packet in it so that I would know when they had received it. They have, but I have seen no response yet."

"May I ask what you said?" Barnabas frowned slightly. He came into the room and took one of the chairs, leaning his elbows on his knees and watching as Jeltor started to pace again.

"You said you know," Jeltor replied, amused.

"The gist of it, yes. You want them to help us with the base. But I'm sure we lost nuance between the translation and the codes." He frowned. "And I'm confused as to why you think they wouldn't offer it when they had already given us intel."

"This would be more...material help," Jeltor explained. "I said that the Jotun Navy wouldn't stand in your way, and that's true. If the Yennai Corporation calls them in for defense, they'll *somehow* manage not to arrive in time. All plausibly deniable, of course."

"Of course," Barnabas murmured.

"It's a good enough plan," Jeltor said.

"Not at all." Barnabas' voice was stronger now. "It's a cowardly plan."

Jeltor gave him a look, and his annoyance radiated so strongly that Barnabas felt it even without looking into his mind. "Not all of us have the strength of the human fleet."

"The Jotun come close," Barnabas argued. "It's well-known in this sector that you shouldn't mess with the Jotun. You don't go around attacking people, but what your enemies start, you finish—decisively. I like that."

"Thank you."

"What I *don't* like—" Barnaba's voice grew dangerous "—is the way you accept the corruption of your politicians."

"We can't do things the way they do. They make the

laws." Jeltor bobbed, clearly upset. "We do our utmost to enforce those laws only in the way that is right."

"The military should *never* be enforcing the laws," Barnabas countered. "The military is there to respond to *threats*. Outside threats. The courts and the police enforce the laws."

"What a strange society you have."

"It's not strange, it's sensible." Barnabas sighed and rubbed his forehead. "All right, leaving aside any differences in how the military works—which would be fascinating to discuss at another time—you're giving your politicians a free pass. No, let me *finish*," he said, as Jeltor's suit crackled to begin speaking. "They've clearly taken bribes from the Yennai Corporation."

"Yes, but—"

"No 'but.' Do you really think that if you simply deal with the Yennai Corporation, those politicians will stop being corrupt? They'll find someone new to take bribes from."

"Oh, no," Jeltor said.

"*Yes*, they *will*."

"Not that." Jeltor's body pulsed and shook. "No, I've been sending them this conversation."

To his surprise, Barnabas started laughing.

"What? This isn't good!"

"It's better than *good*," Barnabas said. "I'm glad they've heard what I said. Now they can't pretend ignorance of their real problem."

"And who are you?" The voice boomed suddenly out of the speakers.

"I'm Barnabas," Barnabas said.

"He's Vigilante One," Shinigami added sweetly. She appeared in the corner, her avatar leaning on the wall, and gave Barnabas a grin. "Formerly Ranger One of the Etheric Empire. He was deputized to enforce the Queen's Justice. In case it's not clear, that's Justice with a capital J."

Barnabas smiled slightly. "With whom am I speaking?"

"This is Admiral Threton of the Jotun fleet."

Jeltor gave a little sound of distress.

"I'm pleased to meet you, Admiral." Barnabas wasn't particularly worried. Jeltor might be correct to be worried, but he guessed that this was going to be an easier conversation than his Jotun passenger thought. "We are both people of action, are we not? I propose we speak frankly with one another."

There was a pause, then the Admiral rumbled, "Continue."

"You've heard my opinions on your politicians," Barnabas said bluntly. "And I'd guess you agree with them. You know that they can't be trusted and that they'd direct you to help the Yennai Corporation when that would be terrible not only for the Jotun, but for many others as well. Is that correct?"

There was a pause, and Barnabas sighed.

Finally, the admiral threw caution to the winds. "You are correct, but—"

"You all say that. No 'buts.'"

Heh. Shinigami grinned at him. *Butts.*

We're negotiating with Jotun high command and you're focusing on the homophone?

Absolutely.

Barnabas resisted the urge to sink his head into his

hands. "I agree that your political system can hardly be overturned in the next few days," he said simply. "However, I *do* believe that standing up for your principles and speaking honestly is a necessary piece of restoring integrity to your political system. Right now, your strategy is to ignore the corruption and hope it goes away. That is one of the most idiotic plans there is."

Most people would preface that with, "not to be rude, but."

I don't care if they think it's rude.

There was a long pause. Jeltor had sunk from agitation into resignation.

"You suggest, in other words, that we help you and bear the consequences," a new voice said finally. After a moment, it added. "This is Captain Qortor of the JFS *Nebb*."

"Pleased to meet you, Captain. And yes, that is what I am suggesting."

"To be frank," the captain said, "it is difficult to see this logic as anything more than self-serving. You will not be forced to deal with the consequences, as we will. Nor do you understand the content of those consequences."

"I believe I do understand," Barnabas said simply. "I have lived many centuries, Captain, both on my home planet and in the wider universe, and I have noticed certain...similarities. There are always consequences for speaking the truth. A government often accrues secrets or has shameful failures, and there is overwhelming pressure for those who see it not to speak of it. Sometimes it is clear that their lives will be on the line if they speak the truth. This is not uncommon.

"But those who care for their society *will* speak up.

They will go with their better nature instead of falling to convenience, and they will stand up for what is right.

"There are those who see extraordinary times and tell themselves that the usual rules do not apply and that no one could blame them for being cowardly. Then there are those who see extraordinary times and understand that extraordinary courage is required of them.

"Believe me when I say that I know the Yennai Corporation is dangerous. I have seen some of their allies and some of their work. They kill those who get in their way, and they make a formidable enemy. Many would say that it is simply enough not to *help* them, but this is not true. If no one stands in their way, they will continue to do evil things. Innocent people will continue to suffer.

"I have made it my personal mission to destroy them. I have already destroyed three of their allies. I ask *nothing* of you that I am not willing to do, myself."

The admiral and the captain had nothing to say to that.

"Do you know what shame feels like?" Barnabas asked. "How it weighs on the soul?"

Jeltor turned to look at him. Even Shinigami was quiet.

"For years," Barnabas said, "I made it my calling to be 'neutral.' I did not intervene in the disputes between my family, no matter how worthy the causes over which they fought. No matter what I do in this life, I will never outrun that shame. If you knew the taste of it, you would do anything to avoid it."

There was a pause, and Shinigami suddenly looked alert. She brought up screens to show a sudden flood of data from the Jotun fleet.

"We can deal," the admiral said finally. "We have intercepted many communications that run through Seres. This is the data we have about the trajectory and encryption patterns. If you can make heads or tails of it, we will be glad to have you deal with the Yennai Corporation.

"And we...we will go to our planet, to work for change. To *demand* change."

Barnabas nodded. "I hope we meet again, Admiral."

"I don't." The voice was wry. "I hope we never have any occasion to do so."

Barnabas laughed. "That, I can understand. I will hope for the same."

22

"This formation makes no sense." In the Yennai Corporation's main base, Wirav stabbed his finger down on the table. He glared at the print-out that showed a plan for how the fleet's ships would protect the base.

"I assure you, it makes perfect sense." Ilia tried not to roll her eyes.

"No! We're not allowed to *shoot* at the ship? This is insane."

"Because we want the ship to be captured without being damaged," Ilia clarified, tensely. Now that she had decided to kill Wirav, she fought for patience. "I need you to *appear* to fire on it and *appear* to protect the base while giving it safe passage to *here*." She reached out to show a glowing point on the model of the asteroid. "They'll think they've gotten in because they're a superior ship. Once they're there, the ship will be ambushed by Zinqued and his mercenaries."

"I don't like it," Wirav ground out. He crossed his arms. "At least let us keep you on one of the ships."

"There's no need for that. We have fifty ships worth of mercenaries that will be on the base."

"Why take the risk?" Wirav asked. He perched on the edge of the table and stared her down. "I can't see any reason that we shouldn't protect you. You're the future of the Yennai Corporation."

Ilia wavered. Wirav's logic actually made sense. She hadn't expected that. Maybe she was being too hasty with her plans to get rid of him.

"And anyway," Wirav added, "*shouldn't* we spend some time together? We are married, after all." He smirked at her, happy to rub the fact of their marriage in her face while the rest of the ship's captains watched.

Her good mood vanished, and she gave him a cold look. "You mean, while the fleet faces down one of our greatest enemies, you would rather be on a date than leading them into battle? Who should we make admiral of the fleet?" She looked around the room and nodded to Gyeir, Wirav's greatest rival. "Gyeir, you're promoted. Wirav, I will send you the paperwork to annul our marriage."

"You would not dare." Wirav slid off the table to glare at her. "Your father appointed me an admiral. Your *father* controls the Yennai Syndicate, Ilia. Not you."

Not for long. Ilia let that thought warm her as she stared at him. "Then do your job, or you'll answer to my father, won't you?"

That gave him pause, at least. He swallowed slightly.

She didn't want to, but she empathized. Her father was one of the most terrifying people she had ever met. When she was very young, he had doted on her a little bit. He still told her about her duty to the company and tested her, but she had been his darling girl and his only child.

Then Uleq had come along.

Their father had pitted them against each other since before Uleq was old enough to walk. Ilia was the first-born, and she was the heir, but her father reminded her at every chance that she could be replaced at any time.

And it was made very clear to her just what being "replaced" meant.

She had been five years old when he'd explained that her uncle was being replaced as the admiral of the fleet, as he had made mistakes during an important engagement. Her father brought Ilia with him to watch the "ceremony"—throwing her uncle off the edge of the Overlook and giving his badge to another.

Even her uncle's wife hadn't dared cry for her husband, not while everyone watched. In the Yennai Corporation, you didn't show sympathy for people deemed unworthy.

Ilia understood, therefore, how worried Wirav was that she would tell her father he was not doing a good job. The consequences would be sudden and dire.

Not, of course, that she intended to be any more lenient with him.

They were still staring at one another when there was a flurry of sound outside, and the door opened to reveal her father.

Ilia gaped. Her heart pounded. Why was her father here?

"Ilia." He kissed her on both cheeks. "Wirav." He gave his son-in-law the same greeting. "And where is Uleq?"

Ilia cursed herself for not having had her brother

executed already. As he had guessed, she hadn't wanted to seem too eager to kill him. If she had, though, there wouldn't be any chance of her father talking to him.

She must not show any fear. She bent her head and tried to look regretful. "Uleq has...destroyed many of our resources. He is at the Overlook while I review evidence."

He stared at her long enough to make her stomach flip-flop anxiously, then looked around at the captains. "Get out," he said. He did not bother ordering them. He did not sound angry. He was simply sure, absolutely sure, that they would obey him.

They did. They knew what he did to people who defied him.

When they were gone, he walked slowly around the table, glancing at Ilia every few steps.

"I'm surprised you haven't executed Uleq yet," he said finally.

Ilia's mind raced. He had given her control over Uleq's case, and if he expected her to have killed Uleq already, then there were a few conclusions to draw. First, that he did not mind if Uleq died. Second, that he might have been testing her to see if she would do what was necessary. Third, that he had no plans to kill her if she executed Uleq, because then he would have no heir left. To her father, his legacy was everything.

She cursed herself for not having killed Uleq the moment he stepped foot in the base, then stopped. All her deductions only applied if her father was telling the truth.

He looked amused as he watched her, and she grew angry. He had always done this: tested her, smirked at her while she tried to find the right answer.

"We have more pressing matters," Ilia said, sidestepping the entire issue. "Uleq has made an enemy of a human ship. It is now coming to find us."

"You know this how?" He looked at her coldly. "No one should know where this base is...unless you have neglected some critical piece of security."

"I have not." Ilia kept her voice strong. She had nothing to be ashamed of. "Uleq engaged the humans several times, first against their Queen, and more recently against this ship, piloted by...one of their generals." As far as she could make out, that was what Barnabas was. "During these engagements, this human ship discovered two of our bases with impressive speed. I find it prudent to assume that they will also find this one."

"So you have called the fleet back." He considered this as he resumed pacing.

"Yes." What did he want her to *say*? She wanted to scream.

"I will be very displeased if this threat is not neutralized, Ilia."

"I am doing what I can to undo Uleq's damage."

He gave her a sharp look. "Do not pass blame, Ilia. Not if you hope to lead this Corporation someday."

But it wasn't my fault! Ilia bit the inside of her cheek to hold the words back. Her father would never listen to them, only think less of her if she pleaded her innocence. She looked down at her hands and closed her eyes in fear when he stopped behind her.

"Ilia. Look at me."

She forced herself to obey him, even though every

instinct said to run. She raised her chin and turned to meet his eyes. He was smiling, to her shock.

"You have never hesitated to do what had to be done," he said. "From when you very small, I knew you were determined. You showed strength time and again."

Ilia said nothing. To relax now could be fatal. Her father's mood could change in an instant.

"I admit I was surprised to hear that Uleq was still alive," her father said. "But not displeased."

Fool, FOOL. Ilia raged at herself. She should have killed her brother. Anything other than having her father be glad to see him.

"It speaks well of you that you do not deal too coldly with your family," her father said. He gave a distant sort of smile. "Not because our family should be above justice, Ilia. That is not what I mean."

She frowned.

"No, it is because those who follow us…are weak. They are lenient with their own families. If we were to do what must be done without any hesitation, it would unnerve them. When your uncle had to die, I made sure to have a trial. I had the evidence shown and appeared to be making a decision. I had known he was guilty from the first day, and that he must die. But the others who commanded the fleet required all the pageantries of that trial. I am glad that, young as you were, you absorbed that lesson."

Ilia managed to smile. That wasn't what she remembered from that day, but she certainly wasn't going to tell him that. She nodded at him.

"And I admit…" He sighed. "I will be glad to see Uleq one more time before he has to die. He is my son, after all."

Under the long sleeves of her robe, Ilia clasped her hands together until they hurt. She should be glad that her father agreed with her about Uleq's death, but instead, all she could find in her heart was sadness.

All her life, Ilia had wanted to win. She had wanted to be the favorite child.

Now she was about to get what she wanted, but *this* was what she'd win—a father whose show of love was a last hug before execution.

It was probably best that she was going to have her father killed, she thought.

But that didn't alleviate the hollow feeling in her chest.

23

"I have something for our next chess match," Barnabas told Shinigami. He directed one of his pawns into place.

She arched one black eyebrow. "A special new form of cheating because you can't win otherwise?"

"Demonstrably fallacious, Shinigami, and you know it. And no. It is..." He reached into a bag by his chair and pulled something out. "This."

"What. The hell. Is that?"

"A chessboard," Barnabas explained innocently.

"It's..."

"A *manual* chess board." He reached into the bag again and pulled out a carved stone piece. "Made specially from the stone on High Tortuga. I commissioned it before we left the first time and was able to pick it up when we were there a couple of weeks ago. Don't you like it? It's a gift."

"I am a holograph," Shinigami said icily. "I cannot pick up chess pieces."

"I'll move them for you." Barnabas smiled. He was

doing his best to look innocent, but there was a faint gleam in his eye. "And you know what's best about this chessboard?"

"*What?*" Shinigami ground out.

"Since there's no way to hack it, there's no way to cheat!"

"That's a lie. There's sleight of hand and camera manipulation. You just mean it's something *I* can't cheat with, you bastard."

Barnabas was laughing now. "I would *never* use this to gain a dishonorable advantage over you."

"Oh, no? You wouldn't? You're clearly not Barnabas, then. Who are you? What have you done with him, you son of a bitch?"

Barnabas grinned as he slid a piece into place. "All right, I *might* have stumbled across some of your latest cheating programs and decided to stave that off a little."

"There is no way you could have 'stumbled across' them. How the hell did you find those?"

"So you do have them. You admit that."

"Son of a—" Shinigami scowled and transformed her avatar into Baba Yaga. "Listen up, ingrate!"

"*Ingrate?* I'm hundreds of years older than you, young whippersnapper, so don't speak to me like you're the grandma. Although I must say..." Barnabas grinned wickedly. "You're not aging very well." When Shinigami's face got stormy, he laughed. "I'll be damned, that works on female AIs, too."

"If by 'works,' you mean, 'makes them want to put crushed up glass in your food,' then yes, it works beautifully." She leaned back in her chair, frowning at him, and suddenly sat bolt upright. "Jeltor. You used *Jeltor* to get into my programs."

Barnabas started laughing again. "All's fair."

"You let him into an Empire AI?"

"Oh, please, those programs were hidden on a partitioned server with no encryption. You'd been using Gar to store them for weeks. Once I figured *that* out...I just had to get to them. And since you had Gar keeping the only access module *you* knew of to get into it, I had to get creative. Jeltor's suit can modify its hacking tip."

"Sneaky bastard," Shinigami grumbled.

"Mm-hmm. Are you going to make a move, or should I just declare myself the winner?"

Her eyes glowed. "Try it, and I'll teach you a new meaning for the word 'pain.'"

Barnabas only snickered.

***

Tafa was painting when Barnabas found her later.

The ship had been headed toward the Votayett system for about a day while Shinigami and Barnabas worked to figure out where the actual Yennai base might be. Gar and Jeltor prepared for the battle, but since Tafa would not be fighting, she had little to do *other* than paint.

When Barnabas entered the room, he paused on the threshold, and she turned to see him looking at her latest completed painting.

"What are you doing?" she asked finally.

He looked at her. "Shinigami has access to certain pieces of my neural networks, and I've asked her to show me your paintings close to the way you might see them. She shows my brain the input of one picture coming through one eye, and the other coming through the other eye. It isn't exact, of course."

Tafa tilted her head to the side curiously. "Wouldn't it be? That's how I see them."

"Because humans have both eyes pointing forward, they use the variation between the images received to create depth perception," Barnabas explained. "Even when we see two totally different images, our brains try to make sense of them in a different way than yours does. I've tried shifting the images to my peripheral vision…but I admit that just gave me a headache. Regardless, they're beautiful."

"Thank you." Tafa smiled. She looked around and was very aware of the mess she had made in this beautiful white room. "Would you like to come in? It's terribly messy, but perhaps—"

"You should see the workshops our engineers have," Barnabas said with a smile. "And, yes, thank you. I came to see how you were doing."

"Well enough, I guess." Tafa fluttered her fingers in the Yofu equivalent of a shrug. "There's not much to do."

Barnabas said nothing, watching her quietly.

"I mean, I'm painting, but…something's missing." She cleared her throat. "I don't suppose you could sit over there."

"Why—oh." Barnabas took his chair and moved it to her side. He still faced her, but now she could see him with one eye. "This takes some getting used to."

"What's it like to see only one thing?"

"Much less interesting, I think, than seeing two things."

Barnabas smiled. "Though I suppose I couldn't say for certain. It sounds like a philosophical question that would be quite impossible to answer."

"I hate philosophy," Tafa said with a shudder. "Mustafee always loved it. He'd quote it at people before he had them executed." Her voice was low and resentful. "He wanted everything he did to be justified, but he was only ever doing it for himself. He enjoyed being cruel."

"I know," Barnabas reassured. He remembered, with unpleasant vividness, the taste of Mustafee Boreir's thoughts. "He was...well, he won't be missed, I don't imagine."

"Only by people who also need to be brought to justice," Tafa remarked succinctly. She looked at one of her paintings. "I think he's what's missing, though. I spent so much time worrying about him that now I don't know what to do with myself. My parents...had a cause. They really believed in something. I was so concerned with my own survival that I didn't have anything like that."

"Perhaps you'll find one," Barnabas offered. "But art is its own cause, don't you think?"

Tafa swung her head so she could see him first with one eye, then the other. She frowned unsure if he was joking.

"I'm quite serious," Barnabas said. "I told you about the manuscripts."

He paused and considered.

"One of the things you practice as a monk," Barnabas said, "is making everything you do a devotion."

"Devotion?"

"A prayer." He considered. "More than a prayer—a service to God. Do the Yofu have deities?"

"Not like humans, I don't think. It would be too complicated to explain. I know what a deity is, though, for other species."

"Very well, then. Prayer is sometimes seen as a dialogue, a request made to God. Then when people do something extraordinary and devote that act to God, or proclaim that they do it to glorify God, they see that as something different than prayer. But a devotion, in the way a monk would perform it, is to do every task of daily life as a… meditation. To do even the littlest thing as if it is for the glory of all creation. Tending a garden, washing dishes, keeping livestock." Barnabas nodded to the painting. "Creating art."

"I do not worship your God," Tafa observed.

Barnabas smiled. "Neither do I. Not in the way a monk would, at any rate. My understanding of things is somewhat different from theirs."

"You were a monk, but you did not believe as they did?"

"It is…complicated." Barnabas took a deep breath and let it out slowly. "I am not just a human. I have changed in ways that some would say mean I cannot worship God. I do not believe that, but it also propelled me to look beyond one view of things. To understand further, I think you would need rather more information about human society than you probably want." He smiled.

Tafa laughed. "I don't understand Yofu, let alone humans."

"I think that would be the honest assessment of anyone speaking about their own species," Barnabas agreed. "Any sentient species is filled with contradictions."

Tafa pulled her knees up to her chest and smiled at him.

She could not remember having a simple conversation with anyone like this in years. She had always been afraid that the people she spoke to were spies from Mustafee, or that he had hidden recording devices somewhere. If she said the wrong thing, she would be punished.

To be able to indulge in a conversation without that fear was a luxury she had never expected. Expectations, after all, led to hope—and she had known since her parents were taken that hope was the most painful thing.

"Tell me about this piece." Barnabas nodded at the finished painting.

Tafa bit her lip as she stared at it. "When I was very little, my parents took me to see my mother's home. She was born in the southern hemisphere, very different from the north. Where she was from, it was all blue hills and scrub brush, and when the sun set, it would be gorgeous every night. We stayed in her parents' house."

Barnabas looked at the painting. He did not speak, only waited for her to explain further.

"I think it was probably on that trip that she rediscovered her belief of…" Tafa sighed and searched for the word. "Peace? Not having weapons."

Barnabas nodded.

"For years, I did not think of it at all, though it is one of my happiest memories. My mother—" she pointed to a piece of the blue image, which somehow seemed to pulse with energy despite being only part of an abstract swirl "—came alive when she was there. I remember her smiling all the time. For months after that, things were different. She was filled with purpose, and she and my father fell more in love than they were even at the start, I think."

"It hurt to remember it," Barnabas suggested.

"Yes." She looked at him and tried not to cry. For a moment, she hung her head and squeezed her eyes shut. "If they hadn't gone back, they wouldn't have...gotten into that mess. Gotten killed. That's what I told myself, anyway."

"You know that's not necessarily true."

"Yes." Tafa clenched her hands, the dual thumbs closing over one another. "And I know it's not their fault, as much as I wanted it to be." She looked up to see Barnabas staring at her curiously. "It doesn't make sense, does it? Mustafee and my aunt wanted to destroy us. They put my parents through things that no one should ever have to suffer. I should have blamed them. But they had all the power in my world, and the more I think about it, the more I wanted it to be my parents' *fault*. I wanted to believe that they had done something wrong, rather than the whole universe is messed up and evil people have all the power."

There was a silent moment.

"Anyway, that's the painting. That trip. I don't want to hate my parents anymore for being tortured or being killed. Missing them hurts so much more." Tears welled up in her eyes. "But it's the truth. Hating them was...believing a lie. I'm done believing Mustafee's lies."

Barnabas reached out to clasp her hand silently, and after a moment of surprise, she closed her fingers around his.

"I know how difficult it is to grieve," he said. "And how much easier it is to take solace in anger. But you're right, it's better, to be honest."

There was a small crackle in the speakers. "Am I interrupting?" Shinigami asked.

Barnabas looked at Tafa, who sniffled and shook her head. "No."

"That's a lovely painting," Shinigami told her. Her tone was a bit awkward, as if she were trying to be nice and wasn't quite sure how to do it.

That made Tafa's heart feel like it was going to burst for some reason. These people might go around wreaking utter havoc with missiles and guns, but they were some of the nicest people she'd ever met. She wasn't sure how that made any sense at all, but it was true.

She had friends, for the first time in her life.

"Thank you, Shinigami."

"Yeah," Shinigami said, still awkward. "Big B, we have a location lock on the base."

"I'll be there in a moment." Barnabas practically leaped out of his chair. He smiled at Tafa. "I look forward to seeing the rest of your paintings."

"Sure." Tafa smiled, picked up her brush and started painting again.

Could art be a worthy purpose in life? She was intrigued to find out.

24

A day and a half passed on the Overlook, and that was enough time for Crallus to learn to *hate* the sound of the reactor below. Food was brought—not much of it—and once or twice, the guards peered through the door as if they wondered if they could get away with beating the prisoners.

Crallus would almost have welcomed that, at this point.

When the door slid open again he felt his heart leap, but he didn't look. Let them try to sneak up on him. They'd kill him if he fought back, but he knew they'd kill him anyway. He'd get in a good fight before they took him down. He'd make them hurt. He'd—

"My son."

Uleq's head jerked up, and Crallus looked around sharply as well.

Torcellans, apparently, didn't age—at least if this one was anything to go by. He looked dangerous and beautiful in the way Crallus imagined the monsters from his bedtime stories did when he was a child. Koel Yennai looked like the sort of monster whose very words would steal your soul. Crallus could see the echo of his features in Uleq's face now.

Everything about Koel made Crallus want to be anywhere but here. Ilia was the type of threat he could understand: cunning, cruel, ambitious.

Koel was something else entirely. Crallus couldn't even guess at his motives. His power, however, showed in every movement he made. It wasn't the sort of power that made Crallus want to challenge him, or even obey him.

Crallus just wanted to run. Preferably all the way to another universe where Koel didn't exist. The very poor second option was to get as far away from here as he could and hope Koel's reach never got long enough to find him.

"Uleq." Koel swept forward, holding out his hands, and Uleq took them and stood.

"Father." His eyes searched Koel's face. "Why are you here?"

Koel smiled. "You do not plead for your life. I like that. My brave son. My *proud* son."

Uleq could not hide his pleasure, but he looked down rather than meet his father's gaze.

"You have always been of great use to me," Koel said. He smiled at Uleq as he spoke.

Crallus watched the two of them silently. Something was wrong here…

"I am glad to have been of use." Uleq had found his voice at last, though it was rusty. "I hope…I will continue to be of use."

His father only smiled at him, rather than answer the

question that hung in words: *will you have me executed? Your own son?*

"Ilia was a fine heir," his father said. "I could tell from the start. She is strong-willed and intelligent. She does not let paltry morals concern her. From the moment I held her in my arms, I knew she would be a fine legacy."

Uleq said nothing. His jaw clenched, and a muscle jumped in his cheek.

"And then you were born," Koel continued. "She was jealous of my love because both she and I knew what you could be."

Uleq kept his head down, but Crallus could *feel* how much he wanted to look up. When Uleq had spoken about how much he hated his father, Crallus had not pictured this. That Uleq would kill Koel if given opportunity, he had no doubt.

But it was clear, also, that Uleq worshipped this man. If he killed Koel, it would only be an attempt to take his father's place.

Crallus didn't know what to make of that.

"Once Ilia knew she had a rival, she became determined to eliminate you." Koel sounded amused. "She tried to kill you that first night, did you know?"

"Yes," Uleq said evenly. "She told me."

Koel threw back his head and laughed. "She would."

Even Uleq was smiling somewhat, and Crallus looked between the two of them with wide eyes. What was going on here? What sort of family *was* this? He and his brothers had hated each other at times. They had always competed to be the favorite. But all their fist fights and petty little tricks had never been designed to do anything more than knock a few teeth loose.

"I knew if Ilia could not control her hatred of you, she would not be a fitting heir," Koel confessed. "There was nothing more important to her. I had to know that she was not going to…lose her head. My heir *must* be strong, not just against others, but against their own poorer nature."

Uleq looked up now, and Crallus saw the hope that the younger male tried to tamp down. *Does this mean you've deposed Ilia? Does this mean I will inherit, that I won't die here?*

"And she has done so," Koel said finally. "I expected you to be dead by the time I got here. She told me how you had failed us. I put your fate in her hands and waited to see what she would do. She wanted you dead…but she waited." He nodded. "She will, indeed, be a fitting heir."

"But—" Uleq's voice broke.

"You have served a great purpose," Koel expressed. "This test did not simply prove Ilia's worthiness, it made her *more* worthy. Trials make us stronger, do they not?"

"Father, do not—"

"Trials make us stronger, Uleq, do they not?"

"Yes, Father." Uleq swallowed.

"And she has one more trial." Koel nodded to himself, his eyes distant. "She hates you, of course, but she also loves you. Having stood strong against her hatred, she must now face the trial of killing you. Only when she has resisted both sides of her weakness will she secure her place."

"*Father.*"

"You have helped to build this legacy," Koel said. "The Yennai Corporation will flourish because of your service."

Uleq's mouth hung open. "You cannot... You came here..." His face set. "You came here to gloat! To tell me that I'd lost."

"To tell you that you have made something that was already great, into something greater." His father's smile was sincere and, as far as Crallus could tell, entirely mad. The older Torcellan actually believed, he saw now, that Uleq should be grateful to die to make Ilia more ruthless.

Crazy fucking bastard. Crallus stared at him, totally frozen in shock. He had served some of the worst people in the universe...he thought. He had become inured to all the cruel things people could do to one another...he thought.

He'd known absolutely nothing. He could see that now.

"I love you very much," Koel said to Uleq. He kissed his son on the forehead. "Die in peace, Uleq. You have been everything I hoped for in a son, and more."

He left without another word, and only when the door closed did Uleq move. He slumped to his knees on the floor, swaying. "He..."

Crallus shook himself, startled out of his daze. He cursed himself. He should have tackled Koel over the edge of the Overlook. What had he been thinking? For the first time, he understood the speeches he'd heard from their human nemesis.

Some evil should just be removed.

"I'll make him sorry," Uleq said now. His eyes were still distant as he began to laugh. He laughed and laughed until tears ran down his cheeks. "I'll make him sorry. I'll steal everything from him."

It's over, Crallus wanted to say. *There's no way we can win now.*

But he didn't know how to speak to Uleq over the sound of this crazed laughter, so Crallus only sat down near the buzzing sound of the reactor and tried not to think of anything at all.

Koel strode through the hallways of the base with a smile. He could not have asked for more from his children.

One of them had always had to die, of course. That was just the way of things. Only a foolish leader would leave more than one heir to rip the organization apart by dividing people's loyalties.

Uleq was enough his son that he would always fight for control, of course.

And Koel meant what he said. The fight had made Ilia stronger. Uleq had performed a vital service for the future of the organization.

He was surprised to see Ilia waiting for him at the launchpad. "Daughter."

"Father." She smiled. "You're leaving so soon."

"I have matters to attend to. I will look forward to hearing word of your victory." He smiled at her so she would be sure to see the compliment in his implicit assumption.

"Ah." She looked vaguely disappointed.

"What is it?"

"I wanted...to show you the AI core." She smiled at him. "This will give us a new form of control over the humans—and over many other governments, I am sure. I wanted you to be here when we first saw its capabilities."

Koel's brows went up. She was right; it would be a very satisfying moment.

"I shall come back, then," he said. "Send word when you have it."

Her smile was a tiny echo of his, cold and self-satisfied. "I will. Goodbye, Father."

Zinqued whistled as their ship came within viewing range of the Yennai fleet. Carriers, destroyers, and a series of frigates hung in a dazzling array. From the charge in their engines, they had only just reached the rendezvous point themselves.

There was a fuzz of sound, then the displays on their screens were replaced by a Torcellan male's face. His hair was worn in an elaborate set of braids, and he looked very self-important in a deep blue uniform that accented his silvery skin.

"Which one of you is Zinqued?"

"Me." Zinqued nodded to him.

The Torcellan did not look impressed. "I am Wirav. We will be bringing your ships to the base, as you were told."

He gave a small gesture to someone off screen, and several of the ships moved to take up position, each hovering over one of the mercenary ships. Tow rods extended and began to lock onto the ships.

A moment later, the electronics all flickered on Zinqued's ship.

"We've lost location tracking," Paun reported worriedly.

"Yes." Wirav looked unmoved. "The location of the base

is not something you should concern yourself with. We will proceed there, you will do your job, and you will be compensated before we tow you back to this point. Are there any questions?"

Zinqued shook his head, and the screens went dark again.

"I don't like this," Paun repeated, and despite himself, Zinqued found himself agreeing.

He looked over, troubled. "Neither do I. But there's no backing out now, is there?"

"No," Paun said finally. "Not anymore."

25

"We're coming up on their fleet," Shinigami reported.

"How many ships?" Barnabas asked curiously as he rolled his neck and swung his arms.

He'd told Gar that a proper warmup was very important. Gar, however, could think of nothing more than leaping out of the ship and immediately dispensing his kung-fu moves. He'd get halfway through a warmup exercise, get lost in thought, then flail with pent-up energy.

Barnabas gave him an amused look.

"Didn't you ever get really excited to beat people up?" Gar demanded.

"No," Barnabas said.

"Like hell," Shinigami snapped. "I saw your vital signs when you were staring down Lan. You wanted to turn that fucker into paste.

"I don't know what you're talking about," Barnabas replied loftily. "And focus, Shinigami. Ships?"

"I can't see them yet. I assume we'll be in sensor range in—WHOA. Whoa, damn. They have a *fleet.*"

"What does that mean?" Barnabas stopped moving, halfway through sliding one of his knives into its sheath. He looked up at the speakers. "Shinigami? Break off if you need to. We'll find—"

"One moment." The artificial female voice was back, and a moment later, smooth jazz came over the speakers. "Thank you for your patience. We look forward to taking your call."

Barnabas rolled his eyes and finished sheathing the knife.

"Any idea where in this base Ilia will be?" Jeltor sounded curious. "Do you think she and Uleq will be in the same place?"

"Uleq may already be dead," Barnabas pointed out. "If your intel is correct."

"My gut tells me that it is," Jeltor said confidently.

Barnabas tried to refrain from asking which part of Jeltor was his gut, and how that was distinguishable from any other part. He was about to break down and mention it when Shinigami saved him by coming back over the speakers.

"Okay, here's the deal, lads."

"You are *not* calling us that."

"No? 'Shinigami's Lads.' I like it. In any event, *lads*, I looked at their communications, and I found the *strangest* thing. One might wonder, who are they waiting for with so many ships? Did they think we were bringing friends? What's going on here? Don't worry, your fearless leader has the answers."

"You're our fearless leader?" Barnabas questioned. "Really? You?"

"Don't make me prove it. I *will* do so." She paused for effect. "*Anyway.* They are, in fact, just waiting for us, and they're planning to make a big show of missing us with missiles, not quite trapping us. We're supposed to think that we made it into the asteroid just because we're so good at flying, and...yeah. Not sure what their plan is from there."

"I mean..." Gar looked at Barnabas and Jeltor as if he thought this might be a trick question of some sort. "Presumably, some sort of trap, yes?"

"Well, yes. But what *kind* of trap?"

"The kind where they try to take the ship without damaging it at all, while presumably also dealing with me," Barnabas asserted. "Which means overwhelming force, likely drawing me away from the ship so they can get to you." Barnabas paused and looked around. "Do your strategic algorithms say the same thing?"

Shinigami grumbled.

Barnabas raised an eyebrow.

"All right, that was a more complete assessment than I expected, with more solid reasoning than I expected." She sounded grumpy. "So, what do we do about that?"

"Well, I don't want to tell you how to run your life," Barnabas said, grinning as he finished putting his greaves in place. He stood. "But I'd suggest that this would be an excellent time for you to use that flamethrower."

There was such a long silence that Barnabas, Jeltor, and Gar all looked at one another in worry. When Shinigami finally spoke, her voice practically shook with excitement.

"Hell. Fucking. *Yes.*"

"The ship has appeared, and we are beginning our firing sequence." Wirav's face was tight with displeasure. "They are evading all of this more easily than they should."

"What does that mean?" Ilia, walking quickly toward the landing bays where the mercenary ships were being offloaded, stopped so suddenly that some of her guards nearly ran into her. She stared into the communications unit, glaring at Wirav. "I told you they were not to be—"

"I *know.* You also said they were to believe they had done all of this through their own skill, which means we have to make enough of an effort that they think we're trying." He sounded like he very much wanted to yell at her. "It would have been better not to have the whole fleet here," he added. "Now we run the risk of—"

"Excuses?" Ilia asked coldly. "Speaking doubts in front of your captains so that if you fail, you can blame me for your own incompetence, Admiral?"

Wirav fell silent, flushing.

Finally, he started again. "What I was saying is that this ship is far more maneuverable and responsive than it should be. I know of no species that can pilot this well." His voice was ugly, twisted with his hatred, but he kept it quiet, at least. He did not look at Ilia.

Don't worry, Wirav. We won't have to put up with one another for much longer.

"Perhaps it is being piloted by the AI," Ilia suggested. "Did you think of that?"

His head jerked up, and he stared at her. "Who in their right mind would trust an AI to fly a heavily-armed ship?"

"The Etheric Empire." Had he not been paying attention to any of this?

"And you want to let this thing onto your station?"

"We can *manage* it," Ilia snapped. "We have hundreds of mercenaries. We can partition and disconnect the AI core. This plan has been approved. Do your piece of it."

She disconnected the call and swept into the main hangar bay.

The mercenaries noticed her, their interest showing in a ripple across the room. One of the Hieto forged his way through the crowd to stand in front of her, and she recognized him as Zinqued.

She smiled brilliantly. One of her father's earliest lessons had been to smile as if every person you spoke to was your most treasured ally. "Zinqued. It is good to meet you."

"And you." He nodded deeply, almost a bow.

He was reserved. She only just kept her eyes from narrowing. He was not pleased to be here.

"Tell me, do you have any questions for me?" She drew him aside, away from his compatriots. Let him speak freely. She would acknowledge his concerns and make him think that he was heard.

It cost her nothing to pretend.

But he only smiled. "No questions," he said. He pointed to the exits that she had predetermined. "We will have one-third of the forces hide within each of those hallways, while my team remains in place on the hanging platform. Once the pilot and crew have been drawn down one of the

NATALIE GREY & MICHAEL ANDERLE

hallyways, they will be attacked, and a second group will cut off their escape. The third group will wait in reserve unless they are called for."

Ilia approved. It met her criteria for dealing with enemies—show overwhelming force, and weaken their resolve as new waves showed up every time they battled their way through. It was always best to make the enemy lose heart.

"Good," she said. "I will remain in my offices. Let me know when you have captured the ship."

Missiles streaked nearby, and the *Shinigami* wove through the spread easily.

Now that she knew the fleet's plan, it was easy to pretend that Shinigami believed this was an attack. She would hold her responses so that some missiles came close, and she made a point of jerking the ship out of the way awkwardly at times as if she hadn't noticed some missile or another.

But between her scanners, her reflexes, and the fact that they weren't really trying to shoot her down, she could have done this in her sleep.

Everything going well? Barnabas asked from the shuttle bay.

Shinigami watched as each destroyer disgorged another spread of missiles. She would have shaken her head if she had one. With the Boreir Group done, these ships really shouldn't be wasting so many missiles.

Then again, they wouldn't last long enough for that to matter. She chuckled to herself.

Yes, everything is going well. Here's the kicker: so our cloaking doesn't hide us from them perfectly, but what it does do is mess with their missile targeting. We're too visible on the one hand, and not quite visible enough on the other. You gotta love it, really. With a surge of inspiration, she charted a path that wove between the missiles and left them colliding with one another. *It's a pity you can't see this as I can. It's amazing.*

Indeed. Between you and Tafa, I've become aware that human sensory systems are quite lacking. He sounded amused.

You're not wrong. Shinigami quite liked Tafa's paintings. *But even Tafa can't see in every direction at once. She can't fly at these speeds or feel the missiles explode.* Feel *the paths she charts...* She waited, but Barnabas didn't respond. *Hello?*

I was trying to imagine it. He sounded almost wistful. *It sounds incredible.*

It is. She launched her own set of missiles and laughed as the Yennai missiles tracked them, only to have hers split into multiple autonomous pieces. *Gotcha, bitches. Time to make you run some defense.*

They didn't like holding back, she could tell that much. She wouldn't push them too hard, for fear that they would lose their tempers.

But she couldn't let them have *all* the missiles-and-explosions fun.

They grouped up for one last attempt at play-acting, and she readied herself. She could see the entrance they wanted her to use now: an isolated landing bay that probably had plenty of space nearby for soldiers to hide.

A lot of soldiers now, a lot of crispy soldiers later. She couldn't wait to unleash the flamethrower on them.

Dozens of full spreads of missiles came out of nowhere, and Shinigami realized the fleet captains had truly lost their tempers. It went against every instinct of theirs to let a ship through their ranks.

She could respect that, she supposed. She just had to make sure she didn't blow up first. She wove through the missiles, looped back, ducked, and skimmed through their fleet so that their ships had to dodge their own missiles.

She was more maneuverable than any of them here, and she reveled in it. They were relying on the slow reflexes of organic life forms.

Their problem, not hers.

She gave one last loop over a few ships to lose the last missile spread, then she slipped into the landing bay of the asteroid.

We're here.

You sound...pleased? Barnabas was still learning her moods, but he hadn't quite assessed this one yet.

Oh, I am, Shinigami said. *I don't know if it's going to be on the way out of here or sometime in the future, but we're going to face that fleet—and I'm looking forward to showing them my true capabilities.*

In the shuttle bay, Barnabas turned to Gar and Jeltor with a smile.

"Ready to get rid of these bastards?"

"Ready." Gar gave the nod.

"Ready." Jeltor's mechanical body stuck up both guns in an approximation of a thumbs up gesture.

"Ready," Shinigami added over the speakers. "Flamethrower primed."

The doors opened, and Barnabas' eyes began to glow. "Then let's bring these bastards to Justice."

26

"You'll find them down any of the three tunnels," Shinigami reported. "From the scans I was able to get as I came in, the far-left hallway leads into a long corridor that runs to the heart of the asteroid. Meanwhile, I believe the people trying to steal the ship are hovering above me."

"What's your plan if they never get in range of the flamethrower?" Barnabas headed for the hallway farthest to the left.

"Turn on the engines, flip them off my top, and *then* hit them with the flamethrower."

"Well, it seems like you have this planned out. Good hunting."

"Good hunting," Shinigami echoed.

At the entrance to the tunnel, Barnabas turned to look at Gar and Jeltor. He put one finger to his lips and held up the other hand to tell them to stay where they were.

Then he started to run. He kept to the outside of the first bend in the tunnel and activated the grav technology in his boots just as he came around the corner. The soldiers, all of whom had been listening to the steps approach, were still aiming their weapons at chest height as he soared into the air and pushed off the wall a few feet above their heads.

He flipped as he came down toward the back of the group, drawing his Jean Dukes Specials. Two shots with his favorite ammo blew whole groups of the soldiers back.

There was a shocked pause, then the soldiers screamed their fury and charged.

Barnabas slid into action with a feral grin. His first task was to clear the small group of soldiers still in the back. He pumped three more shots into one edge of the line and holstered the pistols, drawing his knives instead.

He cut through the group with the sounds of their screams in his ears. His thoughts were drenched in their hatred, radiating from them so strongly that he could hardly close his mind to it.

Sometimes he felt fear or shock, but not now. No, these were well-trained and hired to kill. They'd planned an ambush with no mercy, and they would not give him any chance to escape this if they could help it.

The second detachment of soldiers approaches, Gar reported. *If we hit them from the back,* we'll *be crushed between two forces.*

Barnabas swore. He ripped off one soldier's arm and threw what remained of the soldier into the main group.

Then he charged, driving his way through the very center of the crowd.

These soldiers had not drilled on infantry formations, and they were not trained in anything more than meeting one enemy head on and defeating them in single combat. Still, there were a lot of them. Barnabas felt strikes and blades glance off him, and once or twice, he heard the report of weapons. These soldiers had decided that it didn't matter if they hit their own comrades, as long as the enemy was defeated.

Gar and Jeltor met him in the middle of the group. Jeltor spat bolts of flaming ammunition from his hands, and Gar laid waste to his opponents with unrestrained brutality.

Gar wasn't *efficient*, not yet. He didn't have enough training. But God help his enemies when he learned to be efficient. Barnabas even spared a moment to watch, open-mouthed, as Gar grabbed one of the Hieto and used the heavily-armored body as a mace to beat several other soldiers.

He's got real style, Shinigami remarked.

Barnabas tried not to laugh as he took up position. The three of them maintained a circle, their backs to one another.

That he does. I'll have to work hard to come up with a style of my own.

I look forward to watching your career. Also, it's too bad we can't keep Jeltor. Maybe we can teach you *to throw fireballs...?*

Mmm. Barnabas pulled out the Jean Dukes Specials again and began firing. Three soldiers skidded away in one direction, and four into another. They picked themselves up as others launched themselves wildly in Barnabas' direction, only to meet more shots that sent them stumbling back.

Increasingly, he saw them look over their shoulders as if waiting for reinforcements to arrive.

Barnabas guessed that those reinforcements had seen what was happening and wanted no part of it.

"Shinigami, tell me if any other groups mobilize."

"Will do, but they're staying put." She sounded like she was laughing. "Smart or cowardly? I can't decide."

"A little bit of both." Barnabas grinned and whirled, the butts of his pistols turned briefly into maces to take out several soldiers. "We're about halfway through this set. I wonder if they'll show up when these are gone."

"Maybe." Gar cut into the conversation. He wore a look of intense focus as he fired his weapons, flipped them back into their holsters, and launched into hand to hand combat once more. "How about this? We'll call you if they do, and in the meantime, you head into the asteroid and find Uleq?"

Barnabas wavered, but he knew it was the smart thing to do. Both Jeltor and Gar were heavily armored and were maintaining their composure—while the soldiers were getting both more tired, and more wary of this fight.

It was difficult to find the will to attack someone who had just taken down several dozen of your fellow soldiers, after all.

He had to let them stand on their own at some point. Barnabas nodded to the two of them and leaped lightly to push off the wall and land behind the group of soldiers. They hardly seemed to notice as he ran off into the darkness, except for one thing: he could feel their relief that he was going for someone else.

This was how places like the Yennai Corporation fell,

he thought to himself. Their soldiers didn't fight *for* them. They didn't believe in their leaders.

When it came to a battle of life or death, that lack of faith was fatal.

He wasn't too far from the landing bays when he came to a door manned by several guards. He didn't give them a single moment to respond to his presence. He flipped through the air, one knife sneaking under the furthest guard's neckpiece to slit his throat. The body fell heavily as Barnabas landed on the other side of the group.

The other guards were still looking at the place where he'd been, and he charged them before they could adjust.

They fell within seconds. He used the dead guard's rifle to knock one of them back into the wall and smashed it into the side of his skull. The rifle wasn't as good a weapon as he was accustomed to using, but it worked well enough for him to direct two bursts apiece into each of the remaining guards.

They dropped like stones and Barnabas unlatched the heavy door and pulled it open, striding inside. Such a heavy door was very interesting.

He recognized Crallus and Uleq at once. The Shrillexian stood, his eyes widening at the sight of Barnabas. To Barnabas' surprise, he didn't appear eager to fight.

Perhaps it was the fact that Barnabas was coated in blood. Perhaps it was the fact that he'd seen hundreds of his fellow soldiers killed already. Still, it was remarkable.

It was also noteworthy that Uleq was smiling at him. It was a somewhat disturbing smile, Barnabas thought.

"You're here," Uleq said. "I've been waiting for you. Finally, I get to destroy all of my enemies at once."

Barnabas locked eyes with him and forced his way into Uleq's thoughts. He saw some faces he recognized—Ilia and the Torcellan who must be Uleq's father—and many he did not. They were rivals and enemies from over the years, he suspected, each of them cut down in Uleq's quest for power.

There was no question of what justice meant for Uleq.

But Uleq, backing toward the strange glow at the back of the room, pulled a device from one sleeve. It was counting down, and Uleq laughed maniacally.

"Such a small bomb, isn't it? They didn't find it on the scanners when we came in. It would barely have killed one person on its own. But once it touches the reactor..." He gave Barnabas a crazed smile, launched the bomb over the edge of the floor, and let out a triumphant peal of laughter. "You're going to die with me. Ilia's going to die with me. Your ship is going to be destroyed. And my father's legacy is going to be utterly destroyed, too."

Barnabas froze. There was no way to get to the reactor—

But Crallus gave a primal roar as he burst into motion.

"Like hell, you get out of this so easily!" He locked eyes with Barnabas for a moment, then shoved Uleq out of the way. "Kill Koel Yennai!"

And then he was gone, tumbling over the edge. Barnabas raced to look over the edge.

Crallus was strong, but the reactor was made to power entire cities. Crallus crawled his way to the bomb and smashed it to pieces, scattering the inert fragments of it across the floor before he collapsed.

With the last of his strength, he pushed himself onto his

back to look at Barnabas. His lips moved, and his last thought made it into Barnabas' head:

You have to kill Koel.

And he was gone.

Barnabas turned to Uleq, who stared at the edge of the floor in horror. He hadn't planned to live this long. With his bomb gone, he had no idea what to do. He looked at Barnabas, almost pleadingly.

"There is no need for a trial here," Barnabas told him. He moved quickly, grabbing Uleq by the throat and held him above the floor. "You know what you have done. You will face the consequences. Tell me just one thing: *where is your sister? Where is your father?*"

In regard to Koel Yennai, he found nothing. Beyond a terrifying sense of duty, Koel had never shared his business with his children; Barnabas cast those memories aside for now. The map to Ilia's office, however, formed itself in Uleq's head, and Barnabas took it without any gentleness.

He crushed Uleq's throat, dropped the body, and set off at a run for Ilia's office.

Like hell, she was going to escape.

27

Ilia watched in horror as the human and his companions cut through the mercenaries like they were nothing. Mercenaries rushed them, trying to sink knives into their skin, or shooting wildly, past caring if they hit their own, but nothing they did made a difference. The three figures whirled and shot, deflected hits with reflexes beyond anything she had seen, and it seemed they barely had to look in the direction of an opponent before their target was dead.

She grabbed the communications unit. "Send reinforcements!"

Why was the second wave not converging on them?

The silence was her only answer. She had granted them access to the security feeds, thinking foolishly that this would let them know when they should put the second part of the plan in motion, and where they should go.

All it had done in the end was display the absolute carnage being wreaked by the human and his fellow fighters.

And one of them was... Ilia squinted at the screen. Was that a *Luvendi*? It couldn't be. That was impossible.

But all of this was impossible.

She moaned as she pushed herself back from the desk with her hands over her eyes. She had to find a way to rectify this, or her father would have her executed. There was no possibility that he would be lenient—or even that she could get any of the employees of the Yennai Corporation to follow her, instead.

No one stood up to her father.

She had been the first, the one who planned to shock the rest of them—but she would never get a chance to do that if this all went wrong.

Think, think!

She looked back at the battle, hugging herself. Their attackers cut down mercenaries with brutal efficiency. As she watched, the Luvendi seized a Brakalon and lifted the alien bodily over his head.

Her eyes went wide, and she forgot to breathe as she watched the Brakalon dashed down on the ground, picked up again, and dropped for the second time. The Luvendi hauled his opponent up and hurled him into the group, sending mercenaries staggering and, to judge from the way some of them twitched and went still, crushing the life out of more than one.

Then, one of the strangest things she had ever seen, he made a fist with one hand, cupped it in the other, and *bowed* to the mercenaries he had just killed.

It was only a momentary diversion, of course. He launched into action only a few moments later. Ilia watched him, watched the Jotun...

They had misused the Jotun, some distant part of her thought. She had never known what those suits were capable of. Whenever they met with the Yennai Corporation officials, the Jotun politicians came in awkward tanks that could barely make it upstairs.

And, like fools, the Yennai executives had believed that this was the limit of their skill.

It was now clear that that was not even close to the truth. The suit vaulted into the air, clearly warping gravity and using even more forms of propulsion than Ilia knew existed. Auto-targeting of the arms swiveled to discharge bullets faster than any sentient life form could find and shoot targets on its own. Occasionally, jets of fire shot unsuspecting mercenaries, coating their armor in flames and making them stumble into their own ranks, where the flames only spread.

No, there was no chance the rest of the mercenaries would intervene.

The Luvendi and the Jotun finally stood, panting, in a circle of their fallen enemies and Ilia stared at them, face twisted in desperation and rage. *How?* She wanted to scream at them. *How have you done any of this?*

And where was the human?

Sheer terror buckled her knees. Ilia swiped at the controls to bring up the video feeds. He wasn't back in the hangar bay with the ship. He wasn't cutting his way through the crowds of other mercenaries. She couldn't see him in the Beta or Gamma corridors, and the Alpha corridors...

Those led to her.

She peered along each of the feeds, in turn, whimpering

her fear, and stopped at the feed from the Overlook.

That was Uleq's body. She reached out, her fingers trembling as they dragged across the screen. Uleq lay twisted as he had fallen. Remarkably, his face showed a manic grin. What had happened to him? How had his throat been crushed, and where... Where was the Shrillexian?

The feed outside the door showed only dead guards. Both the Shrillexian and the human seemed to be gone.

There was a noise from behind her and Ilia screamed. She scrambled backward as the human advanced on her, eyes glowing red. How he had gotten into the room, she did not even wonder.

It didn't matter. He was here. He had found the vents, the back doors, the escape routes...

He had found their base when he never should have. Her father would kill her for this failure.

No, wait...he wouldn't. The human would kill her first. A hysterical laugh welled up in Ilia's chest. She could no longer think. The only thought in her head was that she was going to die. All she could see were the red eyes.

"Ilia Yennai." The human's voice was at once mild, and the most terrifying thing she had ever heard. "Do you know who I am?"

"A member of the Empire." She had read Uleq's notes about this man, and they were a jumbled mess of guesses. "Barnabas?"

"That is my name," he agreed. "You may call me Vigilante One. The Empire is no more. I am no longer a Ranger."

Like she even cared about that. A measure of her old anger resurfaced, and she saw his eyes flash.

"You should care who your enemies are," he told her.

Could he read her *thoughts*?

"Of course, I can read your thoughts." He looked halfway between bored and annoyed. "That should be clear from context."

She opened her mouth to scream for her guards—

"They're dead."

Ilia pressed her eyes shut and felt a whimper escape her. This was how she was going to die.

"Yes." Barnabas crouched to look at her. "This *is* how you're going to die: alone, all your money and power useless as a shield, no one loyal enough to try to save you. The mercenaries you bought are thinking better of their bargain. The fleet has dispersed outside, and all communications with them are blocked—you can't call them back. You built up your power in the shadows, and you hid here while you bribed and killed and tortured your way to power.

"And now you've found that in the end, there was no running from Justice."

Ilia's eyes flew open at that. *Justice?* He could not be serious.

"You aren't even close to understanding," she spat. "You didn't grow up like I did, knowing that thousands hated your family and would see you killed for spite."

"Somehow," he said drily, "I find myself more concerned with the people you tortured and killed. You say you were afraid of that. If it was so terrible, why do it to anyone? Think back on them, Ilia. Think of their names. Think of their faces."

She did not want to, but the command was inexorable. She closed her eyes and saw all of them. Her uncle, not killed by her, and yet, she had not spoken up. Her brother, who she *would* have killed if she'd had the chance. Her father. Wirav. The generals who had failed her, and their families. The members of colonies and planets who had opposed her. The loved ones of politicians amongst all species…

"And so many more," Barnabas said, and she remembered that he could see every thought in her head.

He had made her incriminate herself. She glared at him.

"I could have plucked the information from your mind, willing or not," he told her. "I wanted you to remember them. I wanted their faces to be one of the last things you saw before death claimed you."

I hate you. She didn't bother saying the words aloud. She knew he'd hear them.

He only smiled. "Do you even know how much blood is on your hands, Ilia? These are only the faces you remember. Your father built this company, but you did what you could to aid him. You did a *lot* to aid him. You backed pirates and slavers; you bribed politicians and generals to turn on the citizens they were sworn to protect; you had whole colonies wiped out to make way for your mines and your factories. You never saw their faces.

"And it was a choice. Never pretend you were forced. There is no force great enough to compel someone to do such things. There was no ulterior motive, no greater good. You did it for a pat on the head and a chance to have even more power. What more could you want, Ilia? You held lives in the palm of your hand and destroyed them at a whim. What more could you ever want?"

"I wouldn't expect you to understand."

"I don't." He shook his head. "But neither do you. That's the worst part. You don't even know what you wanted. You just killed and killed and killed. You were a force of evil and destruction without even having the decency to care why you did those things. The universe will be better off without you."

She screamed as his knife drove into her heart and twisted. With another scream, ripped deep from within her, she grabbed it and dragged it out. With only seconds remaining, she turned her face to the stone wall so that his face would not be the last thing she saw.

Barnabas stood, looking down at her body.

It's not enough, is it? Shinigami asked.

It's never enough, Barnabas told her. *I stopped believing in heaven and hell long ago—at least, as they're spoken about in the religious texts. But I can see why the thought of them has endured. The idea that she could do so much wrong and just die, not living more than a moment of the terror and pain she inflicted, is an injustice I do not want to let go.*

Shinigami was silent.

But they're dead now, Barnabas said. *There's only one left, and he knows I'm coming for him, I'm sure. He made his children into monsters. I wonder if he'll mourn them.*

From what I know of him, Shinigami said, *from the stories I've heard, I'm not sure he* has *emotions. You thought Ilia was evil? She was nothing.*

Then I will be glad to rid the universe of him. Barnabas cleaned his knife and sheathed it. *What now?*

I thought you'd never ask. Shinigami sounded like she was smiling. *You should come back to the docking bay.*

Are you being attacked? I'll be right there. Just try to hold out.

I don't need your help, Shinigami said, sounding offended. *I need an audience. It's flamethrower o'clock, and this shit is going to be epic.*

Despite himself, despite all he had just seen in Ilia's thoughts, Barnabas managed to chuckle as he headed toward the landing bay. He knew that had been Shinigami's intent, too.

Thank you for keeping me from getting up in my own head, Shinigami. He was careful not to let her hear that.

She would get insufferable if she heard it, after all.

28

Zinqued and his team waited as the *Shinigami* zipped into the landing bay. They watched the captain and his crew disembark and looked at each other in confusion.

A Jotun, a Luvendi, and a human.

It was like a joke. *This* was the crew everyone was so afraid of? They'd freed a whole mining town, fought their way through mercenary bases, and gotten Uleq and Ilia Yennai both so terrified that they approved the hire of hundreds of mercenaries?

It wasn't *like* a joke, it *was* a joke. It had to be a joke. How could any of this be serious? The Luvendi even wore armor.

Zinqued wondered if they just waited for their opponents to start laughing, then shot them all. It was really the only possibility he could believe. Even Paun, world-weary and tedious in his "wisdom" stared at them like he wasn't sure if he should laugh or not.

They watched as the three disappeared down the hallway furthest to the left, and Zinqued nodded at Chofal to be ready. On his signal, she would begin the platform's descent and they would take the ship. For now, they were on a platform painted to look like the rock above, and totally impervious to scanners. They would just wait until the second set of mercenaries moved, then go.

Then the screaming started. Huge booms sounded from the leftmost hallway, almost like a pistol—but what kind of pistol was so loud?

The mercenaries must have some good shit when it came to weapons, Zinqued decided. After all, it *must* be the mercenaries who were attacking. It didn't occur to him that anything else might be the case.

"See if you can get into the video feeds," he whispered to Chofal.

She nodded, and everyone inched across the platform as quietly as they could to watch. When it tipped precariously, they all shuffled into the center, hardly willing to look up even when they might fall hundreds of feet.

The picture, when it came up, was horrifying. The three figures from the ship were, indeed, wreaking havoc.

For starters, the Jotun was not just a blob of jelly in a glass jar. It was actually *fighting*, and it looked like it was fighting well. As they watched, it flipped a knife out of one of its arms, stabbed a Shrillexian that had charged it, then electrified the knife. He screamed and shot back into a group of fellow soldiers, all of whom jerked with some residual current; the knife was still embedded in his chest. As Zinqued's crew all winced in sympathetic pain, the Jotun held out his arm and the knife dislodged itself from the Shrillexian's chest and flew back into place.

The human might *look* like a pile of nothing, but it

ripped soldiers limb from limb. Zinqued even saw it sink its teeth into a soldier's neck and throw the body away with blood streaming down its chest.

"A mentivore," Chofal whispered in a choked voice. There was still a special hatred for any species that ate its own kind, but worse, as far as most aliens were concerned, were mentivores—those who ate another sentient species.

No one had known this about humans up until now, and it was more than a little frightening. What more might they do, after all?

And to top it all off, the Luvendi fought like some sort of nightmare. Had Luvendi been lying to everyone for years? Were they really this strong?

Or was this one…

Everyone looked at one another, imagining strange experiments in laboratories. That would explain everything.

It also meant that no one particularly wanted to mess with these people.

"New plan," Zinqued muttered, very quietly. "The fleet won't attack the *Shinigami*, right?"

Everyone nodded.

"So if we can get on the *Shinigami*, we can get out of here before anyone realizes we're gone."

There was a pause, while they all considered this. They looked wary.

Paun said, "Ilia Yennai is going to have us killed once we've served her purpose."

"And that's if she survives," Zinqued added. For the first time, he was glad of Paun's cautious demeanor. No one would disbelieve *Paun*, of all people. If Paun said something awful was going to happen, you could be sure it wasn't an exaggeration.

Everyone nodded, and Chofal began to lower the platform.

They worked in concert. They knew they had to get the ship before the mercenaries figured out they were running away—because sooner or later, everyone would be running.

And they had to get the ship before the crew got back, too.

"This is really important," Zinqued said, as the platform descended. "We need to pilot it out manually. No computers. As soon as that AI gets online…"

"*Hey.*" One of the mercenaries had come out of the hallways and stared at them. "What do you think you're doing?"

"Follow my lead," Zinqued said under his breath. Much more loudly, he said, "Our part of the plan. *Hide*, the human can't know you're here."

"I don't think so." The mercenary strolled closer. He had his hand on his weapon, and a few seconds later, the rest of his crew flowed out of the tunnels. "I think maybe you step away from that ship and leave it for us."

"But—" Zinqued began.

Paun took over smoothly. He pretended to be confused. "Do you know how to steal ships? Because conventional methods have not worked with this one. That's why we brought you in. With the sale from this ship—"

"It's *us* that put our lives on the line." The mercenary jerked his head at the rest. "We're the ones dying for this. It's *ours.*"

"I don't think you know what you're up against," Paun cautioned. "If you just let us disable its systems, we can sell it, and *all* get rich."

"Maybe we cut you out, and we get richer," the mercenary countered. "And if that doesn't sound like a good plan to you, let me just tell you, in that plan—you get to live. You keep standing where you're standing...and you don't."

Zinqued opened his mouth to complain, and Paun grabbed him by the arm. "I see the wisdom of this plan," he said, with a smile. He dragged Zinqued away and motioned for the crew to come with him.

"Are you *crazy?*" Zinqued hissed. "We're losing a shot at the biggest take we ever had!"

"What are you going to use the money for when you're dead?" Paun shot back. "We lost. The only thing to do now is walk away."

"But...but..." They were *smirking,* all those mercenaries. They looked at Zinqued's crew mates like all of them were nothing.

"I know," Paun commiserated. "But sometimes, you just have to accept that the people who screw you over don't ever pay for it. Sometimes—"

There was a strange roaring sound, and then a scream that made everyone's eyes go wide. The crew of Paun's ship looked around...and their jaws dropped open.

Fire sprayed from flamethrowers on the bottom of the *Shinigami*. The mercenaries, who had crowded close to the ship as they looked over their stolen haul, screamed, and ran for the exits. A moment later, bullets started spraying them.

"This way!" Chofal yelled. She dragged Zinqued and

Paun with her as the crew stumbled for the relative safety of the corridors.

"Why aren't they following us?" Zinqued yelled. Despite the direction of the bullets, all the mercenaries seemed to be trying to escape directly into the line of fire.

It didn't make any sense at all, until…

Until they came around the corner and he realized they were in the hallway the human and his crew had taken.

"*Ruuuuuuun!*" Zinqued yelled as they all turned around and prepared to run toward the death ship.

"Too late!" Paun managed to choke out.

Zinqued and the others stopped. They turned, as one, and met the eyes of the three aliens they hoped to never meet. The human was dripping blood, the Luvendi barely even looked winded, and there was a little pilot light going on the Jotun's suit.

Zinqued tried not to fall to his knees in sheer terror. He was a Shrillexian, he told himself. He needed to have some self-respect. If nothing else, he was *not* going to die on the ground, crying like a baby.

At least the human seemed to kill quickly.

The human crossed the space between them with long strides. "*Why were you here?*" His voice seemed to boom around the cavern. Those eyes, a strange blue color like Yofu skin, stared into Zinqued's. "Ah," the human said. "You wanted to steal my ship."

He could read minds. The room blurred, and the next thing Zinqued knew he was staring up at the ceiling. He had fainted.

Barnabas stared down at him and tried not to laugh.

When Shinigami had told him that she was letting the ship thieves escape briefly so she could have a go at the mercenaries, he'd promised to take care of the ship thieves, himself.

Now they were practically shitting themselves. He'd made a Shrillexian faint.

This was a good day.

He peered into each of their minds in turn. Their captain was a sensible alien, someone who was determined to make as good a living as he could without doing anything too illegal. He'd never done anything like sell the crews of the ships he sold. He always let them off at nearby stations. Not great, considering he stole their ships, but not worth a death sentence.

The Yofu mechanic was hardly above school age. She had a cheerful disposition and liked romance novels, and somehow, she'd managed to get this far on a crew of ship stealers without ever firing a gun.

The rest of them were the same: petty criminals, but not murderers or slavers.

"Listen to me," Barnabas warned. "This is the last ship you will ever try to steal. You will take legitimate work. You will no longer take what is not yours. You will change your ways. You will tell everyone you meet that the *Shinigami* is not to be taken. You will tell them what you saw here today." He pointed to where Shinigami was just finishing off the last of the mercenaries. "You will thank your gods that I am not a man who likes vengeance, but one who delivers Justice."

He leaned forward as they gaped at him, and let his eyes grow red.

"*And you will pray we never meet again,*" he finished, letting his eyes glow and spreading the Fear around him.

Zinqued fainted again. The Yofu mechanic shoved her hand in her mouth to keep from screaming. The captain staggered against the wall as Barnabas swept through the group and across the bay, littered with the bodies of mercenaries.

He waited until they were on board the ship and the door had closed before collapsing into tears of laughter. Gar was also laughing hysterically, and Jeltor let out strange mechanical noises that sounded like a very small car backfiring.

Tafa appeared in the hallway. "What happened? Why are you all *laughing?*"

"They actually...they actually..." Barnabas pressed a hand over his stomach. "They actually shit themselves. Oh, God. I am a very, very bad man. This shouldn't be funny."

"You all laugh," Shinigami said serenely. "I'll just pilot us out of here."

"That sounds good." Barnabas straightened up and wiped at his eyes. "Ah. Ah, that was amazing."

"Mostly amazing," Gar corrected. "I feel like I've been run over by a truck. A truck filled with Brakalons. And rocks. If I'd known delivering Justice hurt this much on the back end, I'd have thought twice about it."

"I hate to tell you," Barnabas said, "but tomorrow is going to hurt worse."

"Not possible."

"And the day after *that* is going to be the worst."

"You're..." Gar pushed himself up and stared at Barnabas in horror. He looked at Jeltor, then at one of Shiniga-mi's sensors. "He's kidding, right?"

"Nope," Shinigami said. "Anytime you want me to try to turn you into an AI, I'm happy to do so."

"That's a hard no from me," Barnabas said. To Gar, he added, "You'll get used to it."

"How? I may die!"

"You won't *die*, you'll just be very, very uncomfortable. We'll have to lure you through the ship by tying pieces of food to strings and making you chase them." Barnabas grinned at him. "Go take some painkillers. And Shinigami —back to High Tortuga. Quickly."

"Why?" Shinigami projected her avatar into the corridor to frown at him.

"I need *juice*," Barnabas declared. "We're out."

29

It was the end of the day, and Aebura's was filled with patrons. The species mingled, from tall Luvendi—all trying to look more grumpy than they really were—to more than a few Brakalons, and Ubuara swinging from the rafters and munching on pieces of fruit from the platters Carter always had waiting for them there.

And, in the corner, there was one table full of humans.

"*See?*" Tabitha demanded.

"I don't know." Bethany Anne looked down at the sandwich. "It's good. No, really, it's good. I like it. But it's…it's just a sandwich."

"Oh, my God." Tabitha flopped her head down in her hands

"Kemosabe," Hirotoshi said patiently. "Kemosabe, a bet is a bet."

Tabitha didn't even pick her head up as she fished her wallet out of her pocket and threw him a bill. "Fine. You win. She doesn't understand true genius in food form."

"Maybe you should have had her try the juice," Barnabas suggested.

Everyone looked at him. While he had said he might be back soon, they hadn't heard from him since that message.

"*Hey!*" Tabitha stood up, threw her arms around him, and kissed him on the cheek. "Big B is back!"

"Have a sandwich," Bethany Anne suggested. "They're very good. For sandwiches. And I hear this is a hundred-percent-Coke only establishment, so I don't have to burn it to the ground or anything."

Carter, who was putting another tray of sandwiches on the table, gulped and slid away hastily with a brief, wide-eyed look of appeal at Barnabas.

Barnabas snickered as he sat down between Bethany Anne and Tabitha. "Where's Michael?"

"He said he didn't *like* sandwiches," Tabitha said, in the tone of someone who had just found out that a close friend liked to kill puppies for fun. "Bethany Anne was *going* to persuade him that he should come next time. Then she let me down."

Bethany Anne laughed. "I'm a huge disappointment," she said, from around a mouthful of sandwich. "It's just good I'm not running an empire anymore, or the whole thing would go up in flames. Literal flames. Nukes everywhere." She smiled at Barnabas.

Barnabas pulled one of the plates toward himself and tucked in. Across the room, he could see Gar talking with some of the other Luvendi. They seemed glad to see him. Perhaps things were turning around here now that Lan and his ilk were gone.

As if Bethany Anne could read his thoughts, she smiled

at him. "Things are going well here. This planet is becoming what we meant it to be—a haven."

"I'm glad." Barnabas heaved a sigh. "I...have a feeling that I'll be called away for a while after this. The more I see of what's out there, the more I realize how much hopelessness there is." He looked down at the glass in his hands. "How do you keep so many people around and keep your resolve?"

Bethany Anne frowned at him. "You're not making sense," she said bluntly.

Barnabas heaved a sigh. Nearby, there was a crash and a shout, and most of the people at the table laughed. It seemed there was some sort of dance contest going on between a Brakalon and some kind of alien with six arms. Barnabas gave a distracted smile at the chaos and looked back at Bethany Anne.

"When I was neutral about everything—"

"Which was bullshit." She took a sip of coke.

"I know that," Barnabas said mildly. "It was easier to pretend that everything would work in the long run, though. Now that I am meeting more and more people, getting close to them, hearing their stories—I realize how much injustice there is, and how *much* it hurts people. Don't you ever feel like you can't make a difference?"

Bethany Anne sat quietly for a moment. "No," she said at last. Her voice was strong, and it only grew harder as she spoke. "Running an Empire was soul-sucking. It was like rolling in a pile of shit all day long. I had to give up everything that was important to me. I hated it. But I would do it all again. Anytime there's one less bastard out there ruining the universe, anytime there are people better off when you leave than when you get there, it's *worth* it." Her eyes started to glow, though she kept a rein on her temper. "There are a lot of assholes out there. It's why I was the Queen *Bitch,* not Queen Everybody-Gets-a-Hug. Let it make you angry. Don't. Ever. Let them win."

Barnabas reached out and clinked his glass with hers. "Anytime there are people better off," he murmured. He nodded. "Someday I hope to have faith like yours."

"How do you compliment someone and make yourself sound so superior at the same time?" Bethany Anne shook her head. "You're a snooty asshole, Barnabas. But we love you."

"I wasn't trying to sound superior!"

You're always trying to sound superior, Shinigami weighed in.

"See?" Bethany Anne cocked her head. "And she knows you better than anyone."

Barnabas gave a laugh and took a drink. "This juice is so good."

"Good enough that you didn't tell me there was Pepsi in the basement?"

"A man does what he must to protect what he loves," Barnabas said simply. "Don't ask me to choose between my love for my Queen and my love for this juice."

Bethany Anne snorted.

"Hey." Carter appeared at Barnabas' shoulder.

"What can I help you with?" Barnabas turned to him with a smile.

"Nothing," Carter said, amused. "We just haven't seen you in a bit. I wanted to see how you were." He sat on a nearby bench, wiping his hands on the towel he had hooked into a belt loop. "Did you finish another mission?"

"Ah." Somewhat surprised by the drift of the conversation, Barnabas scratched at his head.

It's called "making friends," Shinigami explained. Now, play nice with the other human. You clearly need coaching with this.

"I did about half a mission," Barnabas told Carter. "You don't take down something that big just by cutting a few heads off the hydra."

Carter just smiled. "If there's anyone methodically relentless enough to pull it off, it's you."

"Thank you for your support. It means a lot. How's Elisa? How are the kids?" Barnabas' gaze sharpened. "Not upset by what happened before, are they?"

Only a few weeks prior, some mercenaries had decided to make a point by taking Elisa hostage, and she had only just managed to hide the children before she was captured.

"They don't know what really happened," Carter admitted. "They think it was just a game of hide and seek. We've decided not to tell them just yet. Maybe when they're older." He shrugged. "Though I hope by then it won't be a story there's any reason to tell. Once High Tortuga is everything it can be...well. And it's not like they'll get very far in life without knowing that their mother is badass."

"You make a good point." Barnabas had heard the story of Elisa sneaking out of the mercenary camp on her own, and nearly killing a Shrillexian in hand-to-hand combat. "I'll bet she doesn't take any backtalk about bedtime."

Carter gave a bark of laughter. "No. No, she doesn't."

Hey, Chief. Message for you. Sending it to your tablet.

Barnabas frowned and held up a finger to Carter. He pulled out his tablet and smiled when he saw the picture that came up on the screen.

"What the *hell* is that?" Bethany Anne asked from over his shoulder. "Jellyfish family reunion?"

"You're not far off," Barnabas told her. He pointed. "That's Jeltor. At least...I think it's Jeltor? No, that might be Jeltor. It's really hard to tell, they change colors."

"You met a jellyfish and named it?" Bethany Anne looked at him like she was a little worried he might need to be committed.

"They're a species called the Jotun," Barnabas explained.

"Super-powerful mechs," John called from across the table. "I've heard about their battle suits. What do they look like?"

Barnabas passed the tablet across the table without comment.

"You have got to be *kidding* me," John said finally.

"Not at all. They shoot fireballs."

John handed the tablet back with narrowed eyes. He seemed to think this was a practical joke of some kind.

"They'd make good allies," Barnabas told Bethany Anne. "They need to clean up a corruption problem, but I figure having allies to hold them accountable would be a good kick in the pants."

"And it's not like humans can really get down on anyone else for having corrupt politicians." Bethany Anne shuddered. "I do *not* miss Earth."

Barnabas laughed. "Well. Carter, it was good to see you. Bethany Anne, likewise. Tabitha—Tabitha's dancing..." He blinked.

"Come on." Bethany Anne elbowed him. "Stay for a while."

Yeah, chief. You can kill assholes any day. Relax. Unwind. The universe will still be fucked tomorrow.

Barnabas laughed and drained his glass. "All right. A few more drinks."

30

"So you have *no* idea where the fleet went?" Barnabas frowned up at the speakers. "Really? None? You?"

"Yes. Me. Really. None." Shinigami appeared in a flourish and swept over to a chair to sit down.

"You have no need to sit, and you're incorporeal, and you still take a chair?"

"This conference room holds twenty people," Shinigami pointed out. "And there are four of us on this ship."

"Okay, that's a good point." Barnabas looked at her. "I just don't understand how they can have disappeared. The Yennai fleet was *big.* They have to fuel somewhere. Someone has seen them."

"It's not out of the question that they have their own fueling stations." Shinigami shrugged. "In any case, I think it's safe to say that it's going to be a long, arduous process of tracking them down and figuring out their location." She looked up as footsteps sounded and Gar and Tafa came around the door.

"Did we miss anything?" Tafa asked.

"You know, you don't have to come to the war meetings," Barnabas said with a smile.

"I know. I like to." She shrugged. "No reason."

"She's basing a series of paintings on you," Shinigami explained. "Character studies of various moods."

"Shinigami!" Tafa flushed. She looked at Barnabas, embarrassed. "I made such a nice one of you and Gar sparring that I thought maybe I could do some other ones. Maybe I could come on a mission sometime to see you enacting Justice."

"No," Barnabas said. "Embedded journalists are already a bad idea. I refuse to have embedded portrait painters."

"I'll wear him down," Shinigami promised Tafa.

"No, you will not. I am in charge, here, and I say that—"

"Shh. Shh, chief." She held up a hand. "We have a whole fleet to find. Don't worry about the portraits right now."

Barnabas sighed and dropped into a chair. He rubbed his head. "Honestly, the best idea I have at this point is to go back to Virtue Station and lean on one of the bankers until they talk."

"After what Gar pulled, you are not welcome there."

"I know. Maybe if I threaten to sic Gar on them, though…"

"Actually, that's a good idea."

Gar smiled. "I'm finally scary. I spent my whole life not being scary to anyone, and I'm finally scary. God, I *love* this."

Barnabas shook his head with a laugh, but he looked troubled. "How the hell are we going to find this guy if he doesn't want to be found, though? Even his children didn't have any idea where he was when he wasn't at the base. If he doesn't—"

"Message coming in," Shinigami interrupted.

Barnabas nodded to her to play it and the screen darkened for a moment before clearing to show Koel Yennai's face. His eyes narrowed when he saw Barnabas.

"Human."

Barnabas said nothing. His brow was furrowed slightly. He leaned back in his chair and waited.

"You have signed not only your own death warrant, but that of everyone you have ever loved," the patriarch proclaimed.

"Most of the people I've loved are dead," Barnabas told him. "Hazard of getting old. The rest can take care of themselves."

Koel's lip curled and he growled, "You are not safe, human. There is nowhere you can hide from me. Eventually, someone you love will be caught off their guard, and I will destroy them. One by one, the members of your family will fall. I will take apart your legacy piece by piece. I will destroy it, as you destroyed mine. I had crafted the perfect heir, and you took her from me."

"Ilia was a living, breathing person," Barnabas pointed out. "She was not solely your creation. And might I add, she had plans to kill you when you came back to take the AI core."

"I taught her well, then." Koel's face did not flicker. "When she could kill me, she would be strong enough to take my place, and I would no longer be fit to rule. My death would be the greatest gift I could give the Yennai Corporation."

"Crazy motherfucker," Shinigami murmured under her breath.

"I will wipe out every human settlement.," Koel Yennai told Barnabas. "I will kill every alien who has so much as talked to a human. I will make sure that no one in the universe remembers your species ever existed. *And I will make you watch all of it before I let you die.*"

The call flickered off, and the crew stared at the screens with their mouths hung open.

"Well, that's convenient," Barnabas said. He looked around at the others with a smile. "Here we were, so worried about finding him, and it looks like he'll come to us."

FINIS

AUTHOR NOTES - NATALIE GREY

WRITTEN JUNE 26, 2018

Thank you for reading Warden! I can only hope you enjoy reading Barnabas's story even half as much as I've enjoyed writing it. Barnabas is an endless puzzle: someone who likes to watch and act deliberately, but who cannot stand idly by when people are hurt; who believes civility is deeply important, but who has a hell of a temper; who is both kind, and just. What Barnabas tells Gar in Sentinel about flaws is deeply true for him: sometimes it is our best qualities that lead us down the wrong path, and finding our way out of that tangle can be difficult.

As always, I am grateful to my readers for their enthusiasm and feedback. Having a cheering section eagerly asking about the next book is an amazing feeling for an author!

Publishing is a team effort, and so a big thank you also to the whole team behind the Vigilante Chronicles: my beta readers, the JIT group, Lynne and her team of editors, Steve and the administrative team, Jeff, Eric, and of course, Michael!

Thank you to my friends and family for listening to garbled stories and letting me interrupt countless conversations with, "I need to write something down!" Thank you to my fellow authors for their advice and support. I have an incredible community around me and I am thankful for it every day.

Sincerely,

Nat

THANK YOU for not only reading our story, but making it back here to the *Author Notes*, as well!

So, I'm sitting next to Joseph (Joey, our youngest) in our home in Texas. He is presently reading Dakota Krout's *Dungeon Born – The Divine Dungeon* which I "asked" him to read.

<Edit Joey Anderle—He tossed his iPad unto me with express intent to get me to foray into the litRPG genre.>

Why? Because he is a young man, off during the summer with only one job and has another forty-five days to go before his sophomore year in college.

<Edit Joey Anderle—There is no way it is just another forty-five days.>

He could be writing! (Or working at another job, or volunteering… you get the picture.)

<Edit Joey Anderle—I was right, it's fifty days! Oh dear lord it's fifty.>

I've suggested he read that particular book because it is

a LitRPG book that I enjoyed and might help him understand the substance of what a LitRPG book is about.

<Edit Joey Anderle—See above.>

As an avid gamer, he practically IS the target market for
the books.

*<Edit Joey Anderle—No correction needed or warranted. I am
adding this anyway.>*

He has done some remarkable work for such a young
guy, and I'd hate to see him dither away his time when he
COULD be writing. ;-)

<Edit Joey Anderle—I prefer to wither but dither works too.>

I guess this brings me around to Barnabas, and how I
see him as a portion of my own personality. That "dad"
part which is always seeing work and striving to better
oneself. Fortunately, there is a balance which must be
maintained and Barnabas (usually) strives to find that
balance.

*<Edit Joey Anderle—I don't know what a "Barnabas" is, but
it sounds like a main character.>*

Impetuous youth? Often not so much.

<Edit Joey Anderle—I got out my chair to read this tyvm.>

*<Edit Dad Anderle—If it is about him, he can move the sun
and stars to read it.>*

That is always the fun with Barnabas and Shinigami in
these stories.

*<Edit Joey Anderle—I just got the last line clarified its actu-
ally a-ok and I appreciate the compliment.>*

We hope you enjoy them as much as we enjoy making
them happen for you.

*<Edit Joey Anderle -S/O to Ms. Gray for making this all
come together. I appreciate your effort.>*

Ad Aeternitatem,

Michael Anderle

P.S. – I was walking with Joseph last night (late—holy crap was it hot and muggy) and asked him what he had read so far this summer. It was only one book.

You will never guess what it was… go ahead…*guess!*

Ready for it? *How to Win Friends and Influence People* by Dale Carnegie.

<Edit Joey Anderle - I believe I should represent my decision by adding that all successful conquerors start somewhere, and as a small aside I'm now flipping through Don't Sweat the Small Stuff, *and* It's all Small Stuff *by Richard Carson. It's all right.>*

*You can find Joey's first book—*Her Royal Runner—*(written and released while he was in high school) Here:*

https://books2read.com/JoeyAnderle

CONNECT WITH THE AUTHORS

Natalie Grey Social

Email List

https://landing.mailerlite.com/webforms/landing/w0k9j4

Follow Natalie on Amazon

https://www.amazon.com/Natalie-Grey/e/B01MYG7K8P/

Facebook

https://www.facebook.com/Natalie-Grey-393234677682987/

Michael Anderle Social

Website:
http://kurtherianbooks.com/

Email List:
http://kurtherianbooks.com/email-list/